DESTRUCTIVE OBSESSION

Tunisia Riant

MINERVA PRESS

LONDON

ATLANTA MONTREUX SYDNEY

ISBN 1 86106 842 5

First Published 1998 by
MINERVA PRESS
Sixth Floor
Canberra House
315–317 Regent Street
London W1R 7YB

Printed in Great Britain for Minerva Press

DESTRUCTIVE OBSESSION

For my dearest husband Philippe,
thanks for the encouragement and support.
A special dedication to you Kevin.
Fondest memories of my late father and sister, James and June,
and a special thanks to Mummy, Naomi, Lynette, Arlene,
David.

Angelique was happy that the day had finally come to an end. After a hectic day in the intensive care unit, she was rather disheartened; not only had they lost three patients, but she had actually witnessed the death of Deline Travers – Deline happened to be one of her favourite patients she had been treating for a few months. Deline was a very beautiful young lady who had been married for almost a year. They were going to celebrate their first wedding anniversary within a few days, and she was hoping to have a big celebration in the Colosseum hall, but instead she ended up in an intensive care unit.

Angelique was surprised when Deline requested that she be present when her son was delivered by Caesarean section, under local anaesthetic. The baby was being delivered prematurely, because Deline had developed an infectious disease that could endanger her life as well as the baby's. She had been advised to have a hysterectomy, after they found out that she had uterine cancer and ovarian cysts, but she refused, and stopped having chemotherapy. Some time later she got pregnant at her own risk, and she determined that she would carry her baby to term. She was totally preoccupied with giving her husband the son he so dearly wished for, and knowing that he would be the happiest man alive she never considered the risk she was taking with her health and that of the baby.

The delivery was easy, and miraculously the baby survived, even though he was prematurely born. Deline was in a critical condition and both mother and son were transferred to the intensive care unit, where doctors fought for her life. Deline managed to hang on to dear life just long enough for her to get acquainted with her son, before she died in the presence of her husband. André was torn apart. He told Angelique that he had tried to tell Deline that her health was more important than any child in the world, but she wanted him to have the baby, it was as if she wanted him to have something precious to remind him of her.

Angelique had experienced some deaths in the past, and often had a hard time understanding how unselfish people like Deline and many others were to pay such a tragic price. Where was the morality in that? She cried her heart out, and as she went on her knees and said a little prayer for Deline, she thanked the Lord for saving Deline's son.

Angelique rushed to her appointment with her doctor, and was totally exhausted when she finally arrived at Monté Carlin Clinic, where she was to get the results of some hormonal tests she had undergone recently. She was in such low spirits that she was expecting negative results, such as she had always had in the past. She thought to herself that there were no reasons to get her hopes up too high.

Angelique and Eric had been trying to have a baby for over five years, and, most unfortunately, medical practitioners had come to the conclusion that they had done everything they possibly could. She had undergone numerous laparoscopies, during which they had found her fallopian tubes to be damaged and blocked; she also had ovarian cysts that needed to be removed. After a series of hormonal treatments and fertility drugs, her cycle became unbalanced, which caused her a lot of discomfort and led to severe depression. On another occasion she was told that she had a retroverted uterus, as if she didn't have enough abnormalities.

Angelique cursed nature for the way she was born. After she had got back to her normal cycle, she and Eric decided that they would try something different, and opted for artificial insemination, which turned out to be unsuccessful because of the state of her fallopian tubes. They then tried in vitro and did five tentatives, and even that didn't work, so they called on the latest invention called the micro injection, where the spermatozoa was injected into the ova after they had been removed from the ovary and then implanted back into the uterus. They managed to have three embryos implanted, and nothing happened at the end of her cycle, she just had her menstrual period as usual, but there was no way she was going to give up hope.

Her psychologist told her that she was too anxious, and that she should put the thought of having a baby entirely out of her mind and find different things to distract herself with. She told her that the majority of her patients who took a break were surprised that they got pregnant without planning it. Angelique left the surgery thinking that it was a load of crap. Doctors had actually told her that she was sterile, and that she should think about adoption, so what was this woman trying to prove? Angelique knew how much Eric wanted to have a child of his own, and she felt guilty about not being capable of giving him a baby. She thought of how unfair life was, and she felt that nature had a peculiar way of preventing things from working out for people who desired to have children, while others practised abortions and child abuse. She often consoled herself by making believe that Eric loved and cared for her in the most exceptional manner, and that he had proven it to her throughout the years they had been battling together. He had promised to marry her some day, whether she was barren or not.

Angelique had been sitting in the waiting room for over thirty minutes when the clerk appeared and showed her to the doctor's consulting room. She was still upset about Deline's death, and trembling.

'Good afternoon, Miss Castelino, how are you feeling today?'

'Very tired, Doctor, I've had a strenuous day, and I'm looking forward to a very calm evening,' she said. 'Have you had the results of the tests?' she asked, almost yawning.

'Absolutely,' he said, with a strange expression on his face. 'We've received the results of your tests, and I'm afraid that you're going to have to listen to doctor's orders, under very strict supervision, you'll need a lot of rest, and I'm going to give you a prescription in the meantime, so you won't be so tired. You're unwell, my dear, but we'll take a closer look at that tomorrow.'

Angelique was stunned, and wondered why he wasn't being more specific. Looking him in the eye, she demanded to know what he meant by unwell.

The doctor told her to calm down and assured her that aside from her positive pregnancy test she was anaemic and needed closer medical treatment, although judging from his examination she was going to be all right.

'Positive? You mean positive pregnant? As in having a baby…?'

'No doubt about that,' he said, 'but before I confirm your pregnancy, I would like to do a sonar scan early tomorrow morning at about eight o'clock, so drink a lot of liquid and don't urinate before coming here.'

She left the clinic thinking about her mum, and what she would've said in such circumstances. Angelique remembered, whenever she had some kind of deception or was depressed, that her mum would tell her that every dark cloud had a silver lining, and that positive thinking was a leading role in achievement. She suddenly thought of her childhood and the happy family holidays they used to spend together, travelling to different islands. Angelique's father was into travelling and touristic communications; he ran a travel agency and got to go to different islands all the time. She remembered the story about how her parents met, and how she was conceived in the Seychelles.

Every year they would go on a six-week vacation, to Mauritius, Réunion, the Maldives, Haiti, Hawaii, Caribbean Islands and many more.

She specifically remembered the last island they visited. They had heard of the Comoros in the Indian Ocean and Angelique's dad wasn't going to miss this one for anything in the world. They arrived in Moroni, the capital of Grande Comore and booked into a five star hotel for a few days. During the day they visited museums and souks. They came across some Madagascan stands at the market place and visited the Third World hospital, Peltier, where people were lying sprawled all over the floor because of the shortage of beds; casualties were very high. Hygiene wasn't a priority and flies stuck to the undressed injuries and wounds of certain patients, who weren't attended to because of the shortage of staff.

The positive aspect about the island was that the ocean was magnificent; they would take a bush taxi and drive for kilometres around the island. They later booked into another hotel in Maloudja, that was about forty kilometres from the city and the airport. They were overwhelmed by the beauty of the black volcanic rock and the white sand beaches.

The hotel they lived in was grandiose. There were all kinds of water sports at the *club nautique*, and they tried out deep sea diving, and did a lot of snorkelling. They were surprised to see that the locals were still using dynamite explosives to fish, and catching a lot of white sharks. They often sat at the sea-facing bar watching dolphins and ray fish in the clear waters of the lagoon, rainbowed by the superb colours of turquoise, blue and green. They discovered a private beach where hotel expatriates lived, and they were given permission to use the facilities whenever they felt like it, so they'd go down to the beach, where they'd have breakfast at the Maloudja hotel restaurant, watching a school of dolphins do their act in front of them.

What was most breathtaking was that the place smelled like jasmine, and vanilla was growing all over the place. There were trees called ylang-ylang, a flower that was made into a perfume and used as incense. They hired a four-wheel drive and drove to the salt lake, they climbed up the volcano, and sometimes watched the locals picking mangoes, pineapples, bananas and pawpaws that grew wild. This was all very exciting, and Angelique had enjoyed herself thoroughly, but duty called, and she had engaged herself with a private tutor and well-known mathematician, and she had to leave, knowing how much her father wanted to make the excursion with a private helicopter which would fly them around the island, and then go on to the adjoining island, called Myote, where they would have landed before going on to other islands as well. Angelique insisted that they continue without her, while she boarded a flight to France, and then back to Maldavia.

Two weeks later she received a telegram, summoning her to the Comoros. She was informed that there had been a plane crash, with six passengers aboard and three crew members. It appeared that the pilot had suffered heart failure and crashed into volcanic rock, killing all the passengers and his crew. She returned to identify her parents, packed up their private belongings, and then flew their bodies back to Maldavia. After the funeral, she was terribly lonely; she had no other relatives, but she had friends and neighbours, who turned out to be very helpful. She got over their death thinking that she could have been with them at that time, and she remembered that they had had a wonderful holiday, and that they died doing the things they liked most. Even though they died a tragic death they had enjoyed their lives up to the bitter end.

Angelique thought to herself that her day turned out to be wonderful after all, but she wasn't going to allow herself to build up false hope that might turn into deception later. So, she would just wait until the ultrasound and then take it from there. She got home, watched a movie, had something to eat, and tried to get some sleep, but she kept on tossing and turning. By six o'clock the following morning Angelique was at the clinic, and seemed to be the only out patient in the area, but she couldn't care less, she was impatient. She tried not to be noticed when suddenly she spotted Doctor Muller coming from the delivery room, but he had already seen her, so he invited her to have a cup of coffee with him. She was so nervous that the doctor decided to examine her straight away.

The ultrasound was underway, and it seemed like an eternity before the doctor finally said something.

'Now, what have we here? Oh, that's great. Come on, Miss Castelino, relax and have a look. Yes, those are the little fingers, this here is the head and there are the little limbs. Let's check out your baby's heartbeat,' he said.

When Angelique saw the graphic going wild she was so thrilled that she wasn't listening to a word that Doctor Muller was saying, but found herself crying with joy. When the doctor had concluded the examination she jumped up and hugged him tightly and left lipstick all over his cheeks. He congratulated her and told her that she was three months pregnant, and that she would need an ultrasound on her fourth month, to decipher the sex of her baby if she wanted to know, and then he prescribed some calcium and iron tablets and told her to take it easy.

Angelique couldn't believe that she was three months pregnant. She had a bloated belly, but that wasn't abnormal;

she had missed her period for a while, but that too had happened in the past. On her way home she stopped at Marcy's supermarket, and went on a wild shopping spree. She hadn't spoiled herself in ages; and she had something to celebrate, so she bought smoked salmon, caviar, big slabs of chocolate chip mints and lots of fruit and vegetables. She was going to have a baby in April and that was hardly six months away. As she entered her superb ground floor apartment, she couldn't help admiring the scenery that seemed more beautiful than ever; even the birds were singing their sweetest lullabies, while lovers walked hand in hand, as if they were sharing the happiest moment in her life.

She changed into a sarong, and went onto the veranda, overlooking the lake surrounded by coconut and pine trees. She was so happy that she could hardly wait for Eric to call. Eric happened to be away on a family vacation with his parents, and Angelique was supposed to have gone along as well. However, when a colleague had an accident, and another was on leave, naturally she was called upon to work, and she couldn't refuse. Eric was very disappointed and wanted to call off his trip to stay with her, but she insisted that he go.

They were to stay at Mountain's Peak for a duration of one month, and she was expecting him to arrive within three days, and as usual she was looking forward to his call. She prepared a meal and dined in the lounge, but Eric didn't call that evening or any other for some time. She called the telecommunications to ensure that she didn't have a problem with her line, and checked the telephone plug. Some days later she received a telegram informing her that, due to bad weather, telephone communication was out of the question, and that they had extended their stay for a further two weeks.

Angelique was relieved that they were safe, but disappointed that she needed to wait for another week or two. Two weeks had gone by, and she wasn't expecting Eric to phone, when she had a call from Eric's Aunt Brumilda, who had just got back from Mountain's Peak. She told Angelique that she could expect them back within about five days. It appeared that Mr Lemoin had a business deal to conclude before coming home.

Angelique went about her business as usual for the next two weeks. She felt rather lonely and didn't have a soul to share her so long awaited joy with. She regretted not having any family; being an only child, she had been left on her own when her parents died. Then she thought about Murielle, her best friend and confidante, in some ways the only family she had when she had to confide in someone. Unfortunately, Murielle still hadn't got back from her fling with the gorgeous Frenchman she was meeting on the French Riviera, where he had a sea-facing villa in Saint Raphael. Murielle had also been gone for several weeks, and should be getting back soon.

When another week had gone by, without a sign from Eric, she started to worry and thought that something was radically wrong, as it was totally unlike him to leave her without even a telegram or a message. Suddenly it occurred to her that the only person who would know where they would be was Eric's grandmother. She dialled the number and got an engaged tone, so she tried later and still got the same tone. She told herself that if she wanted to know what was going on she needed to drive over and find out for herself.

It was Saturday morning, the weather was divine; all she needed was some company to drive up to Marula, where she would spend the long weekend, but Murielle was still abroad. Angelique wasted no more time, and went on her own. She stopped off at the petrol station, filled up her tank and bought some refreshments for the road. She was about to drive off when she realised that the windscreen was rather dusty, and she had a long journey ahead, over four hundred kilometres. She asked the petrol attendant to wash the car. While he was at it she went to get something to drink, when some careless person bumped into her, making her stagger, and spilling his sticky Coca-Cola all over her pretty satin blouse. *What a clumsy lout*, she thought as she looked up, with the intention of giving him a bit of her mind, when for an instant she thought that she was facing Eric. She then realised that it was Antoine, Eric's younger brother, who had been away on a business trip in Asia.

'Hi Angel, how are you babe? I haven't seen you in ages, I've missed you so much,' he said.

'I'm doing great,' she said. 'Nice to see you, you've been pretty scarce yourself.'

'Yeap, couldn't stick around to see my brother take over where I was supposed to be, it drives me insane, you know that I'm the jealous type,' he said, laughing. He hugged her and asked where she was going.

'I'm on my way to Marula, to see Grandma Lemoin, to find out if she knows where I can get hold of my future husband. You know that she knows the whereabouts of everyone. I haven't heard from Eric for over a month, and that's unusual.'

Antoine agreed, and told her that he wouldn't mind coming along too, because he hadn't seen the old lady for quite a while, but mostly because he would get to be in Angelique's company for a long, long weekend. He parked his car at the garage and offered to drive.

During the journey they spoke about old times and how things had changed since then. Antoine and Angelique were at school together and had the same crowd of friends back then. They grew up in the same neighbourhood, even though Angelique came from a rather middle-class family, whereas Antoine's family was exceedingly rich. Antoine was head over heels in love with Angelique, but she had always considered him as a big brother and best friend. They attended social gatherings and parties together, so most people assumed that they were having an affair. Antoine told Angelique about his feelings for her, but she didn't encourage him, and made it clear that they would remain friends.

Antoine never took no for an answer, until they graduated from college and the farewell party was to be held at his parents' home in Calicorne. Everyone was going in different directions to further their studies, and as usual he was Angelique's chaperone. Angelique had already met Mr and Mrs Lemoin on several occasions, and made quite a good impression on them, she was very beautiful, somewhat reserved and very independent. They knew that she didn't feel the same way about Antoine as he did toward her, and often encouraged him to date other girls, but he had no interest in others. The evening of the farewell, Antoine managed to persuade Eric to stay and meet some of his friends. Eric hardly got along with Antoine's friends, but made an exception to attend that specific evening, an exception that Antoine was going to regret in the future.

Something peculiar happened when Antoine introduced Angelique to Eric. They were practically entwined when their hands met, totally besotted with one another, so that for an instant they lived in electric avenue, only coming down to earth when Antoine reminded them that he was present. Antoine knew that something had happened between the two of them, nothing could have been more evident, and he almost regretted having made his brother stay. That evening, Antoine's night, turned out to be a nightmare, while Eric couldn't keep his eyes off Angelique, following her around like a little puppy dog all night long.

There was no doubt about it, it was love at first sight, and any fool could see that the feeling was mutual. They exchanged telephone numbers and started to date. Angelique never meant to hurt Antoine, but she had nothing to feel guilty about, and expected him to be happy for them. Instead he rejected her, and really envied his brother, although finally he did come to terms with it when he realised that there was nothing he could do to keep them apart.

Eight months later Eric and Angelique decided to live together. They found an apartment in Calicorne, close to Eric's family. Angelique had rented out the family home she cherished, but she had so many memories there, and would have felt lonely. Anyway, the place was hopelessly too big for two people. It was amazing that it had felt so full with only the three of them in it at the time. Antoine had decided to leave and travel abroad on business, and finally he became accustomed to Angelique and Eric's relationship, and knew that some day they would wed, and he was happy for them.

When they finally arrived in Marula, after hours of driving, they stopped at a restaurant for lunch, as they had at least another hour before arriving at the castle.

Antoine surprised Angelique by saying, 'I suppose I have to congratulate you Angel, Mum told me that the wedding arrangements were being made and that I had to get my butt over here as soon as possible, to be best man. I'm surprised that you didn't tie the knot a long time ago.'

Angel thought that it was rather surprising that Edwina had told him about the wedding, knowing that she wasn't too keen on the marriage. She knew that Edwina liked her very much, but that she was having a hard time accepting her because she couldn't give them any grandchildren. Antoine told her that to Eric it made no difference, and his mum approved wholeheartedly, and would have done anything in her power to find a solution for her to fall pregnant.

Angelique giggled like a little girl and replied, 'She won't need to do any such thing now, the deed is done, there will be no more excuses of that sort.'

'You're not pregnant, are you?'

'Oh yes, I'm almost four months pregnant, and I can't wait to break the news to Eric.'

Antoine was completely taken aback, as he had resigned himself to Angel not having children. Knowing what she had endured in the process, Antoine couldn't help shedding a tear of joy on Angel's behalf, and just told her how good God was. Antoine's reaction towards the news really flattered Angelique, and she knew that she had his blessings then.

They now had to climb to get onto the road leading to the castle.

Angelique looked ahead and said, 'My word, look at all those cars and people, there must be some kind of function, or funeral.'

Seeing all the cars, Antoine told her that if there was a funeral he would have been informed, it was certainly a private function.

Angelique suggested that they had chosen the wrong moment to arrive, and that there was no way they were going to gatecrash. Antoine told her not to worry, he remembered his childhood hideaway, where he sought shelter when his presence was not permitted, so he drove up his secret pathway and parked under his super willow tree from where they could see everything that was taking place around them.

Antoine told Angelique that it was like the old days when he used to do this as a little boy. When they had finally settled down, they realised that it was a wedding, and it looked as if a princess was getting married. It would be interesting to see the bride, and surely they might know who it was.

After about ten minutes Angelique imagined that she had actually seen Murielle's vehicle, a Lexus open coupé. She double-checked the registration number, and knew she was not mistaken, because Murielle was the only person in Calicorne to have that specific model and colour, and she had her name engraved on her number plate. She wondered what Murielle was doing at such an elite wedding, but then she recognised other relatives of the Fourbourg family, so she tried to fathom out who could be getting married in their family other than Indra. Then she remembered that Indra could most probably afford such an expensive wedding, if she was marrying Pedro de Oliveira.

Angelique found it rather strange that Murielle hadn't told her about the wedding, unless she had only just got back from France. Angelique had always considered Indra a friend, and couldn't understand why she wouldn't want her to know that she was marrying her rich lover boy. It was unlike her, because she often bragged about Pedro, and both Angelique and Murielle sometimes told her to calm down in a jokey manner. She remembered that they met for lunch some time back, and that Indra was in a great hurry and rushed off to meet Pedro, who had something very important to share with her. Before leaving she had promised to tell them about his announcement without delay.

Angelique and Antoine sat on the bench, as if it were a planned picnic, while they nibbled on the rest of the take-away, envying the wedding guests, who were going to sit down to a decent meal within a short while. Angelique consoled herself by telling Antoine that there would surely be some leftovers when the reception was over. They had a magnificent view from where they had parked. Angelique noticed Fabian getting into Murielle's car. He looked outstandingly handsome and was dressed to kill. Some other people joined him to reverse some cars, making space for the oncoming vehicles, including limos, and one could hear the procession and the church bells ringing as well. Suddenly two red limousines pulled up one after the other.

From the first limousine, there was no doubt, Mr and Mrs Fourbourg appeared, waited on by two neatly dressed doorman, who opened the doors to let them out. They were followed by four absolutely stunning bridesmaids, carrying the most beautiful bouquets of pastel colours matching their skin-tight peach-coloured silk gowns. It looked like a real fairy tale. They assembled as if they were having photographs taken, while Murielle stood proudly beside her mum, scarcely visible. She seemed to be timid and Angelique tried to get a closer look but she just couldn't be sure if it was Murielle or not, although from a distance it certainly looked like her.

Pedro's family were led from the second limousine, and followed by four gloriously dressed ushers, all dressed in black tuxedos, with top hats ribboned with pastel peach and carrying canes. It was a pity that the audience made it difficult for them to get a better view. There was a crowd of people surrounding the family as they came closer, so that it was extremely difficult to catch a glimpse of them.

When Antoine noticed how excited Angelique was he joked with her and said, 'When you get married it will be something out of the ordinary, because you'll have the most unusual wedding having such a glamorous best man as myself; you'll have even the queen to attend, not only all the little princesses in the world.'

Just then a white Cadillac pulled up and a big fuss was being made. Angelique was very inquisitive and wanted to see what Indra looked like. She made herself comfortable. When the bride stepped out of the Cadillac and walked closer towards where she was standing, she saw the bridesmaids carry the four-metre long trail, and the bride seemed taller than usual, undoubtedly because she was wearing high heels. Indra looked perfect: she wore a white satin and lace wedding gown with puff sleeves, and the bodice was full of diamond sequins, while a diamond crown topped the veil covering her face. Her husband joined her and pulled it aside, and surprisingly turned his back almost immediately.

Angelique thought that they were behaving in a rather peculiar manner, but she was in for an even bigger surprise when she noticed that it was actually Murielle and not Indra's wedding. Angelique was even more confused when she realised that she had mistaken a bridesmaid for Murielle, while she was the actual bride. She couldn't believe that her best friend, who had pretended to be in France, didn't have the decency to tell her that she was getting married.

There was something tricky about this wedding, she thought. Why hadn't she been invited to the wedding? If Murielle had nothing to hide, all this seemed unreal. Angelique was so disappointed, it was most incomprehensible. She wept because it didn't make any sense at all. Murielle and Angelique had been best friends for over fifteen years and they knew every secret about each other.

When Murielle had broken up with Paolo about three months previously, she was the first to know. Angelique knew that Murielle wasn't seeing anyone else in particular, though she mentioned that she had met someone who had a crush on her, but it wasn't serious. If Murielle had reconciled with Paolo, why was it such a secret? Angelique had known that Paolo never appreciated her and even accused her of being a bad influence on his girlfriend, but she didn't realise that he disliked her to the extent of getting Murielle to break their precious friendship. It felt like a slap in the face, and Angelique felt cheated on and abandoned. Angelique called it a day thinking that she had much more important things to consider than crying over spilt milk. She was going to marry the man of her dreams, and she was expecting his child, and she would have shared her good fortune with Murielle. She thought to herself that she wasn't welcome, and that she didn't want to waste any more time, it was much too painful to watch, so she made a suggestion to Antoine about driving up to the holiday inns in Marula centre, and coming back when the party was over.

While Angelique spoke to Antoine, she noticed a strange impression on his face, as he stared at the bride and the groom. She asked him what the matter was, but he just nodded his head and instructed her not to look. She was certainly not going to obey, so she took a closer look and noticed that the groom looked very familiar, and it was certainly not Paolo. Then he removed his white top hat and turned toward the crowd.

Angelique fell to the ground, landing on the hill and rolled down the slope, right down to the fish pond where people were accumulating to congratulate the newly-weds. She rolled right up to the feet of the groom. While Antoine made his way down to rescue her his first concern was for Angelique, but as soon as he saw that she was out of danger, he turned to the groom, and smashed his face to a pulp, causing him fall into a puddle of mud. There had been a struggle, and the bride came running over to see if her husband wasn't injured, but she too was in for a big surprise. By now Angelique had gained consciousness and had gotten to her feet. She walked right up to Murielle, who still looked decent enough at that time, slapped her across the face and sent her sprawling to join her husband in the muddy puddle. She was unable to utter a word, because of the shock, while Antoine picked her up and led her away from the scene, leaving a doctor to take care of Eric's bruises.

Eric had suffered numerous bruises, a fractured and deformed nose, a dislocated elbow and two fractured ribs. Murielle looked on to a blood and mud-stained husband, who was being carried away on a stretcher to an awaiting ambulance. Murielle herself looked like a crying puppet, with a smudged, messed up face, which made her look as if she was a Rolf Harris painting. Murielle had black mascara travelling down her cheekbones, that blended with the foundation to leave her in a total mess. Her pure white satin gown had turned into a brown potato sack, while a journalist captured everything live.

The Lemoin family didn't want any reporters present, but the Fourbourgs had insisted on publicity, so they got their money's worth, and there was entertainment for everybody – there were even television broadcasting corporations and elite newspapers.

As soon as they reached Calicorne, Antoine called a doctor to examine Angelique, who cried her heart out. He was afraid that she might have injured the foetus, but the doctor assured Antoine that the baby was just fine and that he had given her a sedative that would calm her for the night, although he needed to do a sonar scan the next morning to be on the safe side. Antoine thanked the doctor, and saw him to the door. Antoine was uneasy and decided that he wasn't going to take any chances, he would get her to the nearest clinic for safety measures. When they got back to Angelique's apartment, he spent the rest of the evening at her bedside.

The following morning, while Angelique was still asleep, the doorbell rang, and Antoine found himself confronted with a journalist. At first he hesitated, and then granted an interview, not that he wanted to be seen, but he felt that getting things off his chest would make him feel better, and people would realise exactly what sort of brother he had.

Dave Kline from the magazine *Gossip* asked Antoine to explain why he had acted with violence toward his brother, on his wedding day. On his wedding day? Antoine replied that Eric was officially engaged to be married to Miss Castelino whom he had been living with for six years, and that he had just eloped with her best friend. Antoine told him that he felt like killing Eric and accused him of being a low class spoilt brat, and a double-faced liar. Antoine maintained that Eric used people to achieve what he wanted, and nearly always succeeded.

'He managed to entice Angelique at a time when she was vulnerable, knowing how much pain and humiliation he was causing me. Eric is a manipulating bastard who gets away with murder using everything and everyone to achieve his goals in life at the expenses of other people's feelings. He used Angelique to get to know her best friend and then eloped with her and finally married her. I hate him, and never want to speak to him again. He needs to leave Angelique in peace from now on, if he doesn't want to end up paying very expensively for the humiliation and pain he has caused her.'

'Are you in love with Miss Castelino?'

'Oh yes, since we first met I fell in love with her, and I'll always love her, but the feeling isn't mutual. She sincerely loves my brother and I know that I don't have much of a chance. If only I knew that I had even one chance, I would leap at the opportunity, but I know that I'd be fighting a losing battle. Eric doesn't have the faintest idea of what love means. She sincerely loves him, and obviously it hurts to be cheated on the way she has. Eric deserves what he gets, he deserves to suffer. He will never find peace and happiness in his entire existence. Eric won't ever find peace of mind, and I wish him the worst marriage on earth.'

Just then he heard Angelique screaming, and rushed to her side. She had been having a nightmare. She started recounting that she had dreamt about a wedding where she had slapped Murielle for marrying Eric.

She added that it was a ridiculous dream, but Antoine assured her that she wasn't dreaming, but that one day Eric would pay for the hurt he was causing her. He took her into his arms and told her to cry her heart out. She still didn't realise what had hit her. Antoine knew that she was going to need an eternity to get over this heartbreak, and he vowed to be at her side whenever she needed him.

Eric was watching the evening news bulletin and realised that the incident was making headlines on every channel, as well as in the newspapers. He watched his fairy-tale wedding turn into a nightmare. Eric's dad, Alex, was at his hospital bed at the time, and told him to understand why Antoine was as angry as he was, and that if it had happened to him under the same circumstances, he would have reacted in exactly the same manner. Eric understood, and knew that he probably deserved the hiding he got from his younger brother, but there was no way he expected to be demolished.

After they had spoken about an eventual peace pact between themselves, both Alex and Eric burst out laughing about it. In the meantime, Edwina didn't think that it was funny at all, but there was very little she could do at the present moment, so she kept them company for a while and left. Murielle had just entered, and Alex excused himself. Eric allowed her to stay for a while and then asked her to leave, because he needed to rest.

Antoine stayed with Angelique for several weeks, until she felt strong enough to make it on her own. He persuaded her to move out of her apartment, and find a house in Calicorne with an option to buy later if she felt like it. After considerable thought she came to the conclusion that Antoine's idea was fabulous and she wasn't going to waste any more time. Moving would permit her to get her mind off the memorable years that they lived in apartment number thirteen that turned out to be unlucky for some. She eventually found a beautiful home, and she moved in straightaway, leaving strict orders with her ex-landlord not to furnish her residential address to anyone at all, although she left him with a postbox number, where he could forward remaining correspondence.

She was now comfortably installed in her new home, and rather liked it. Antoine called on her as often as he could, and she seemed to have come to terms with her loss, but she still became depressed when she thought about Eric, and she certainly had something that reminded her about him all the time. Antoine was very supportive and never ever mentioned Eric's name.

Eric and Murielle moved into a double-storey mansion, offered to them by his parents. Murielle bragged to the entire neighbourhood that she had chosen the furniture and that they did plush wall-to-wall carpeting in their home. She often told her hairdresser, Salome, that they were happily married, knowing that Angelique had her hair done at the same salon, where people would surely keep her informed about the latest news concerning the newly-weds, but she didn't know that Angelique no longer went there.

Angelique had frequent calls from her ex-landlord, informing her of the people who enquired about her. He told her that on several occasions Eric had called and begged him to furnish him with her address, but of course he had refused.

Angelique got used to having Antoine around, and he was a great help. He spent all his spare time with her, and even accompanied her to her antenatal classes. Sometimes she would laugh when people complimented them on being a great couple, obviously thinking that Antoine was the child's father. He participated in everything right up to the eventual delivery. Angelique was very thankful that he was so supportive and concerned about her. Frankly, she didn't know who she would have turned to if Antoine hadn't been available.

Angelique was seven and a half months pregnant, and she had not seen Eric since he married Murielle three and a half months ago. She couldn't help wondering if Murielle was pregnant. Since the wedding had taken place, it was rather strange that Angelique hadn't taken time to think why Eric suddenly married Murielle, after he had asked her to marry him some days previously. None of it made any sense. She thought about the evenings she worked night shift, when Murielle offered to keep Eric company, or even cook for him occasionally. She remembered Eric telling her that he preferred being alone, and that he could tolerate Murielle's presence, but didn't really like her.

What a confounded liar he was, and she actually believed that he didn't like her. She had trusted them with her life. Angelique realised that they must have been having an affair for a long time and she was too ignorant to see it, and what must have happened in the process was probably that she got pregnant so he was forced to marry her. Angelique still couldn't understand why he told her that he loved her and that he would never exchange her for the world, and that he wanted to spend the rest of his life with her, whether they had children or not. The Lemoin family looked happy with the arrangement of Eric's marriage to Murielle, which meant that even Grandma Lemoin was a liar too. She had gone as far as to remove a diamond ring that belonged to her grandmother, saying that she wanted it to be refurbished for Eric and Angelique's wedding; she had always welcomed her into the castle and treated her like a family member. Angelique tried not to torment herself with something as simple as the fact that Eric married Murielle because he made her pregnant, thinking that she couldn't give him the child he dreamed of, but she couldn't forgive him for not telling her about it, and cheating on her with her so-called best friend.

Antoine came around for a chat one day and they decided to go out to purchase the baby's layette together. Antoine was totally thrilled that Angel had asked him to come along and help her choose some tiny little things. They went over to the Baby's Parlour and had so much fun, just looking at the tiny little bibs and crawlers. Earlier, they had seen the doctor after Angelique had a sonar scan, and decided that she wanted to know the sex of her child. She was overwhelmed when the doctor announced that she was having a boy.

While Antoine was joking around holding up a blue crawler, and pointing to a blue pram, Indra walked into the store and greeted them. Indra was unable to hide her surprise, seeing Angelique in the state she was, and being with Antoine, who seemed to be thrilled about having a baby boy, judging from the colours they were choosing. She congratulated them both, and told them that she would never have thought that they would actually end up being together. Both Antoine and Angelique laughed at her statement and decided to leave it at that.

Indra was very excited that she finally had something interesting to tell Eric and Murielle about, so she did not waste a second and drove over to tell them the news. Unfortunately they were out, so she was forced to return on another occasion. Later that evening, Indra couldn't wait to see the look on Eric's face when she told him that his brother had made a better job of things with Angelique, taking over where he left off. Indra had not been on good terms with her sister since the incident; she had refused to attend their wedding, so it was quite surprising that she should call on them, but it was her way of paying them back for the hurt they had caused Angelique. She beat around the bush for a little while.

'Did you know that Angelique and Antoine are having a baby?' she asked.

Murielle replied in a very sarcastic manner, 'You've got to be kidding,' almost certain that Indra was taking her for a ride, but Indra told her that she was out looking for a christening present for Maureen's daughter, when she ran into Antoine and Angel.

'They seemed to be having so much fun. I'll even tell you that they're having a little boy, because they chose only blue and white.'

Indra emphasised how good Angelique looked, and that she was radiant, even though she had put on a lot of weight. Indra could see that it was the most painstaking message Eric had ever had to hear. Eric enquired about how far Angelique was in her pregnancy and if she was fatter than usual. Indra laughed at Eric's childish question, and told him that she was massive; there was no doubt that it was a multiple pregnancy in the way she carried.

Eric had tears in his eyes, and refused to hear any more details. He got up and left without saying a word and slammed the door behind him.

Murielle told Indra that she was aware that she had a crush on Antoine, but it would be better if she steered clear, because she had no chance. Indra retorted that she was a real bitch and that she was looking out for her own egotistical satisfaction and had no respect for other people's feelings. She had her reasons for marrying Eric, and she had better watch herself, because it wasn't going to last eternally. Murielle told her that with Angelique pregnant she had a good chance.

Eric rushed over to his mum's place, and needed to tell her what he had just heard. When Eric arrived Edwina was, singing away, while she was baking his favourite, apple pie with cinnamon.

'Hi Mum, you look as if you've won the lottery, how are you today?'

'Couldn't be better,' she said, surprised to see Eric, almost out of breath.

'Where's Dad?' he asked.

'Your father's busy organising a party. He has just been cleared of all the allegations, and there's a warrant out for the arrest of Luc Fourbourg, who seems to have disappeared. I would like to see the look on all their faces when they pick him up within the next few hours,' she laughed. 'They also found Mr Durand's body buried in some rubble on the site, that is very sad indeed, it's a real pity that he had to die because of a financial scheme, but Luc will be looking at a lifetime for an extra charge of manslaughter.'

Eric hugged his mum, and told her that it was great news, but that he had other great news for her. 'Congratulations, mother dear, you're going to be a grandmother.'

Edwina, very surprised, told him that he was crazy, she wanted to know how he could have gone to bed with such a manipulating person like Murielle, after all the damage she had caused. She told him that he was welcome to father her child, but should not expect them to accept a Fourbourg in their family. Eric just laughed and told his mother that she was highly mistaken and that he would never touch Murielle with a six-foot pole, even if she happened to be the last woman alive.

Edwina was totally confused; if Murielle wasn't pregnant, then who did he get pregnant? She wanted to know who the person was, slightly agitated. 'I thought that you were going to try and patch up things with Angelique.'

He looked at his mum, and said sadly, 'So did I, but it appears that it's too late already; she's pregnant and carrying Antoine's baby.'

Eric told his mum about Indra's visit, after she had met Antoine and Angel at Baby's Parlour, shopping for their baby boy. It appeared that they were having loads of fun, picking out prams and baby clothes.

Eric was in tears when he confided that he had imagined that it would take for ever for Angelique to get over him, but it seemed that she didn't waste any time either. Antoine was so proud, but if that was her way of taking revenge, then she really had managed to break his heart; but he couldn't blame her, after all, he had married someone else without even giving her an explanation. Mrs Lemoin stopped him, and told him that it was impossible for Antoine to be the baby's father. Eric demanded an explanation.

'Do you remember, when you boys were about ten and eight years old, Antoine took part in the junior horse jumping championships, and had a nasty fall; his boot got stuck to the saddle, and the injured horse dragged him along for quite a distance and then they fell into a ditch – Antoine's little body was beneath the horse? He was badly injured, and on arrival at the hospital he had an emergency operation; his manhood had been crushed, and doctors already knew that he would need several operations to correct the problem. After his sixth operation further surgery was called off, because he had infections that had spread, leaving him totally sterile. He had therapy for years on end but that too came to an end when they found out that he would never be able to have children. As if he were self-destructive thereafter, somehow he managed to get stuck in barbwire, aggravating the circumstances.'

'Have you told him about this?'

'Of course I did,' she said. 'He suffered enormously, and was completely traumatised, he had finally accepted his destiny, and showed signs of coming to terms with it. One of the reasons why we were very pushy about your having a baby was so that he too could share the joy of being a biological uncle.'

But Eric was even more confused; if Angelique wasn't having Antoine's baby, then *who* was the father of the child? He was going to find out, and break the man's skull for taking advantage of a vulnerable female.

Eric went as far as threatening the landlord, by telling him that he was withholding serious information, and that in a court case he could be jailed. Mr Lanjagger panicked, and immediately handed him the address. He decided that he would call on her later that evening, and he was almost certain that she would bang the door in his face. First, however, he had some serious business to resolve; he had applied for an annulment of his marriage to Murielle, and she needed a medical certificate, to prove that she wasn't pregnant. A few days later, by pure coincidence, Murielle was seeing Doctor Muller at the same time as Angelique, and they all ended up in the same waiting room.

When Eric saw Angelique his heart skipped a beat, and he knew that it was time to break the ice. On the other hand, Angelique stared at Murielle, who was as flat as a pancake, and assumed that she had lost her baby, or that she was just starting a pregnancy. Eric greeted them, and sat beside Angelique. He looked at her stomach and congratulated her, telling her that it looked as if she was having twins, and that she was radiant and looking well.

He was almost furious, when he enquired, 'Who is the lucky man who managed to do what I only dreamed of doing? I cannot leave things the way they are.'

He was almost yelling, and people were looking on, but he just carried on; he told her that he could explain everything and had wanted to for a long time. She replied that they had nothing to say to each other. Eric was in tears when he told her that he loved her, and that he had never stopped loving her. He wanted to make things right, if she would give him a hearing. He told her that he could hardly believe that she was having someone else's baby, when it should have been his. Angelique felt sorry for him, but he had chosen someone else, and that was his own decision, so she made it clear to him that now his responsibilities were towards his wife whom he had married under oath until death do them part. Murielle couldn't agree more, and reminded him that they got married in church. Eric looked at her, and was enraged when he told her to shut her trap before he did it for her. Both Angelique and Antoine were surprised at the tone of voice he was using towards his wife.

Eric told Angelique that he was no longer married to Murielle, and that their marriage had been a marriage of convenience, and if she would just listen, she would understand why he had to marry her in the first place; he told her that she didn't know the half of it.

Angelique was confused and furious. Suddenly she said, 'If you're not married to that two-timing bitch, then please tell me what the hell she's doing here, in my sight? You had better get her out of my way before I commit a crime.'

Eric told her that it was routine to have a check-up, before the annulment of a marriage, and he promised that he was never tempted to touch her, there was absolutely nothing that kept them together, so she was free to leave.

It all sounded like a winner's edge and made no sense. When they were leaving the doctor's, Eric told Murielle to find her way out and that from then on she was on her own and that he didn't wish to cross paths with her again in his entire existence. Before leaving, Eric reminded Angelique how much he loved her, and that he was well rid of Murielle, and that she would have to listen to what he had to say. Angelique refused to listen to any more, while Antoine told his brother to lay off and call it a day. By now even Antoine was amazed at what had just occurred.

Antoine was furious, and said, 'You son of a bitch, I don't know what exactly you are trying to prove, but I'll tell you this much, you stay away from Angelique if you don't want to regret the day we met, because I sincerely think that you have caused enough damage. Right now you're actually pleading for mercy, why should anyone forgive or even trust you? I don't trust you, I never did; everyone you touch ends up being hurt in the long run.'

'I want you to remember something, brother dear, that I would never hurt someone intentionally without valid reason, but this time I had no choice. When you finally find out what happened you'll see why I had put myself into this predicament and lose everything in the process.'

Eric turned to Angelique and told her that he was sincere about loving her, and that he wanted to make things right between them, and that he wasn't going to give up on something he had wanted for so long. Antoine was ready to slap his brother after he had kissed Angelique on the cheek and told her that he would love her eternally, but she managed to stop him just in time.

Antoine wasn't going to leave it at that, he needed an explanation, and he knew someone that could tell him, so he drove Angelique home and went over to Indra's house. When he arrived, Indra and Murielle were having a serious discussion and Murielle had been crying, and gave him the cold shoulder. Before Antoine could address himself to Indra, Murielle had already said what she had on her mind.

'I don't see what difference it makes to you to know what happened. You had better do something to keep her for yourself, especially now that you have managed to get her into your bed and make her pregnant. Everybody knows that you would do anything to keep her, so you'd better find a way to keep Eric away,' she said angrily. 'Personally, I am not willing to let go that easily, so you'd better marry her while she's expecting your child.'

Antoine looked at her and told her what a stupid bitch she was. 'It is amazing how you pretended to be her very best friend, and surely after fifteen years of buddy buddy pretences you should have known better, that Angel didn't sleep with any Tom, Dick, or Harry and certainly not with me, so get your priorities straight and use your common sense for a change – she's having Eric's baby.'

Murielle was so surprised that she almost fainted; she would never have thought for one moment that Angelique was carrying Eric's child. She just howled with anger, and cursed the day she had met Angelique, and wished her bad luck in the future. Antoine had concluded his conversation with Indra shortly thereafter, and left enlightened about the actual events that had taken place.

Antoine didn't bother to tell Angelique what he had just found out until a few days later, when Mrs Lemoin phoned Angelique and asked her if she could come over to have a chat. Angelique told Mrs Lemoin that she didn't mean to be rude, but that she preferred not to have anything to do with them, and that it would be better if they didn't see each other. Mrs Lemoin was a stubborn person, and there was no way she was going to leave Angelique to believe that they deliberately abandoned her. She drove right over to the house and rang the doorbell. Angelique knew that it could only be Mrs Lemoin, so she told the butler to tell the people at the door that she wasn't in, but Edwina wasn't going to have a servant stop her from entering. She walked right in, and told Angelique that what she had to say was of the utmost importance to her and everybody else who had suffered just as much as she had. She wasn't going to leave until the entire situation was clarified.

Within seconds Edwina had got down on her rear end and got seated on the carpet in a very comical position, and both Angel and the butler burst out laughing, and then she joined in. Angel wasn't going to make her leave after all, and helped her up from the carpet, still giggling at the silliness of Edwina, and invited her to have a proper seat if she wanted to be comfortable. Almost immediately thereafter the ice had been broken between them.

Angelique offered her a hot cup of coffee, while Edwina congratulated her and told her that she was very glad to be a future grandmother. Angelique asked her why she was so sure that the child she was carrying was that of one of her sons. Mrs Lemoin told her that she wasn't born yesterday, and that she knew that Eric was the child's father. Edwina told Angelique that she had managed to keep it away from Eric, but she had known immediately.

'If you think you can keep me away from either you or that child, it isn't going to be that easy,' she said. 'I will spoil my grandson to the extent that you would finally have to allow me to see him.'

'How did you know it was a boy?' she asked, almost surprised.

'I have my informers,' she said laughing. 'I have known you for years, Angel,' she said. 'If there is one thing I know about you, it is how faithful you were to Eric. I admit having had doubts about your ability to conceive, but I finally resigned myself to accepting your marriage to Eric anyway. The whole problem started just sometime before we left for Mountain's Peak. It would probably have made a difference if you had come along as planned.

'Alex came home from the office, and was constantly in a foul mood, but refused to talk about it, so I didn't bother forcing him to confide in me. Two days before we left, Alex came home and locked himself in his study, where he made quite a few phone calls. It was very strange, because he never had any secrets, or so I thought, but he was certainly keeping something from me. When I asked him about it, he just replied that it was professional, and that everything was all right.

'We were to leave early the next morning, and Alex had just had another argument with Luc Fourbourg. He poured himself a giant cognac, and that was really unlike him. We drove over to Grandma Lemoin, where Luther awaited to drive us up to the airport.

'We arrived at the Peak, and had a warm welcome by none other than the Fourbourg family in person. Everyone was there except Murielle, who was to arrive within a few days. We were very surprised, and thought that it was rather a pleasant surprise to have company for a while. Alex explained that he had plotted the surprise with Luc, and thought that we would be thrilled. I couldn't understand why he chose Luc and Francisca though; we were never close friends, even though they were associates in business.

'After a few days, Murielle arrived, and there was a party in the recreation centre; all the youngsters went along while the adults played poker. In the meantime, back at Marula, Grandma Lemoin saw to all the wedding arrangements, and had catalogues of the most beautiful wedding gowns you can imagine. Eric had already pointed out the wedding gown you had marked in the *Femina* and she ordered it, as well as the cake you were arguing about – instead of a three tier she ordered a six-tier fit for a queen. Naturally, she was not to let you know that the wedding was arranged for the week we got back.

'We had arranged for Antoine to attend, and then drive you over to the Holiday Inn to have your hair done, and a manicure; you were to be blindfolded while they were dressing you. Antoine was to drive you to the church and walk you to the entrance, from where Alex was to lead you down the aisle to Eric's side. Antoine had even had your grandfather's ring polished for Eric.

'We were all excited about the wedding and told the Fourbourg family about it. They seemed to be thrilled for us, but a few days later I regretted ever having told them about our plans. Not only was Francisca a nuisance, but she was trying to matchmake Murielle with Eric. She continually bragged about how pretty Murielle was, and that it would have been great if she were marrying Eric.

'Eric told her that you were the love of his life, and they were invited to the wedding as well, and he reminded me that we were to print all the invitations and send them out. Francisca found it all very exciting, so she offered to help out with the names on the list of guests. When we had finally listed all the guests, Luc told us that they had business to attend to in town, and that they would take care of the invitations while we ladies went shopping. He was a very shrewd man; he brought back copies of the original invitations and handed them to me; everything seemed in order, he had copies of every invitation we had listed, and the proof that it had been forwarded. Two days had gone by when Alex told us that there were serious problems that he couldn't tell us about, but that we had to postpone our flight for another few weeks. I told him that it was impossible, that all the wedding arrangements had been made, and that we had to leave, but he promised that we would be at the wedding, only that it would be that of Murielle and Eric, and not Angelique.

'Eric couldn't believe what he had just heard; already he'd been thinking of how lucky he was to be marrying Angelique, and now he was being forced to marry her best friend, and he disliked her intensely. Eric made a scene and told his father that he would rather die than marry Murielle. After Alex had explained to us that Mr Fourbourg had already sent out the invitations to both our relatives and theirs, it just didn't make sense until Alex gave me the copies. They had used the exact same invitations only they had changed the name of the bride and doubled the number of guests.

'Eric was in such a state that I needed to calm him down. He refused to listen to his father and threatened to leave immediately, but Alex told us that if Eric didn't marry Murielle he would go to jail for crimes he didn't commit and that being in jail wouldn't prove his innocence. Luc Fourbourg was blackmailing my family and he had enough false evidence to jail both Eric and Alex for a long time before they could prove their innocence. Luc accused Alex of fraudulent manoeuvres by paying Mr Durand to tamper with the ledgers, and of having millions of dollars transferred to different banks abroad, such as the Swiss Bank, the Bank of Monté Carlo, the Bank of Montreal and South Africa's Bank of Lisbon, and all the transactions were in Eric's name.

'Mr Durand was the financial controller, and the books looked as if they had really been cooked, so Alex was framed. Some time back they had a discussion about financing a business in another country; because Luc only had shares in L & F, Alex was the moneybags, so he opted to go and have a look at the possibilities, while Luc had him photographed at each bank, in the company of the financial controller, and pretended that he had hired a private eye when he started suspecting Alex. Then there was the video tape, where Alex and Mr Durand were having a meeting that led to a heated argument, and it appeared that they were arguing about finances, as Mr Durand kept on pointing to the ledgers. Sometime later, Mr Durand had disappeared from the face of the earth, and Luc accused Alex of bribery as well.

'We had no alternative but to accept his terms, hoping that we could nail him in a short while, and prove Alex's innocence. Eric insisted that he wanted to call you and explain things, but Alex told him that it would only complicate matters and jeopardise his plans, as Mr Fourbourg wanted him to break all ties with you, and make you believe that he had eloped with Murielle. His plan had been studied perfectly, but you weren't supposed to have walked in on the wedding, because he had planned for you to read about it in the newspapers. That's why he ensured the presence of *Gossip*, because he knew that you had it delivered to your home. Eric believed that he would somehow be able to explain to you what had happened and he was sure you would understand.

'Luc just didn't give up, he continued to find new evidence that could nail Alex if ever he thought of making the blackmailing public. Then he had found something else as well: he told Alex that he could have him arrested for fraud because some workers had proof that he was responsible for the fire in the warehouse, and said that they had been paid out an enormous amount of money by the insurance company for material that didn't even exist, and that they had all the loading bills to prove it.

'When we finally arrived at the castle, Grandma Lemoin refused to have any part in the wedding. She sulked and didn't say a word, she refused to meet Murielle's family and made no secret that she didn't like them. Alex pleaded with her to understand that she needed to make an effort, that it would only be for one day. She left promising to do her utmost to make the wedding a disaster.

'Instead of pretending, she played some dirty tricks on them. Firstly, while they were at the church, she got the thank you cards removed from the tables and replaced them with heart-shaped cards containing both your photo and Eric's. When they arrived back from the cathedral, Murielle looked absolutely delighted when she saw about four helicopters flying to and fro, trailing a love message for all to see.

With all my love, until death do us part. To my one and only beloved Angelique, from Eric.

'Murielle was thrilled when she saw the message being advertised for the whole of Marula to see. I remember seeing the expression on her face when she said that it was terribly romantic, only to find that the message was intended for someone else. Murielle felt terribly embarrassed when she read a little bit further, and realised that she was being humiliated. Everyone else looked just as confused as she did, as she tried to explain to the guests that there was an error and that it would be rectified immediately, but then her mum came over and informed her about the thank you cards as well. Murielle was furious that Grandma Lemoin had made such a fool of her, though she was not in the least concerned about the consequences thereof. It was a pity that you didn't notice the helicopters, you might have seen that there was something fishy going on at the time,' she said.

'Oh, oh yes I saw the helicopters, but Antoine distracted my attention every time the message appeared, so I never got to see it, and it's just as well, because I would have been even more confused,' she said.

'Eric remained faithful to you; even after the wedding he made her life a misery, he didn't even converse with her. He dined at our house everyday. She had the audacity to call at my home looking for Eric. She rang the doorbell, and I answered. She greeted me politely with a huge smile on her face, but I just looked at her, holding my dry expression so she would understand that she wasn't welcome, and I told her never to set foot on my premises ever again, and that if she wanted to see Eric, she was to stay home and wait for a phantom to return, and I slammed the door in her face.

'She never did come back, and Eric kept to his bargain about not seeing you, but he tried to contact you on numerous occasions. At first I felt sorry for Murielle, being led into such a raw deal, and having to choose between you, her best friend, and her father, but I soon understood that she was very comfortable with the situation. She tried to entice Eric, she actually felt comfortable planning her every move. If she had her way she would have invented a phantom pregnancy as well, but Eric just pushed her aside, and told her that he tolerated her for your sake, but he knew that she was a tramp and he just needed some time to prove it to you. Eric slept in another bedroom, and he consumed all his meals at our place. Murielle had tried everything to turn Eric on, and when it didn't work she despised him, and threatened that he would pay in the long run.

'When they eventually had enough proof about Mr Fourbourg's conspiracy and he was being threatened with a tough jail sentence, Murielle panicked, knowing that Eric was going to annul his marriage to her, so she staged a nervous breakdown, thinking that Eric would feel sorry for her, but he completely ignored her, and walked out. As soon as the police had informed us that there was a warrant out for the arrest of Luc, Eric told Murielle to pack her little rags, and start moving. He told her that when he got back in the evening he didn't want to see a trace of her. A few days later he put the house up for sale.

'Murielle felt that she deserved to keep the house and all the furniture as well as the car and a monthly maintenance, because they were married with everything in joint names, but Eric told her that she was such a stupid gold-digger, that she didn't even realise that she signed an pre-nuptial agreement from the word go. Eric thought that if she was a victim like he was, he would have given her some sort of indemnity or compensation, but she was in this to get something in return, she was a fortune hunter, there was no doubt about that, but she'd been misleading you from the very start, and she used you to such an extent that she laid hands on Eric, thinking that she would eventually get him to sleep with her, she would fall pregnant, and then she would have him somehow. But she never anticipated that he wouldn't even go as far as to touch her, so she told him that she was always in love with him.'

After Angelique had listened attentively, she thanked Edwina, and told her that it would have made a difference if she had known from the beginning, but everything always worked out for the best, and that it was the most unselfish and brave sacrifice a person could make for a loved one. They changed the subject and had already gobbled up so much tea. Angelique called the bakery to order some fresh cream pastries to be delivered, when the doorbell rang. The doorman opened up and informed her that Mr Antoine, accompanied by his elder brother, was here to see her, and it appeared that another car had just pulled up.

Angelique got the butler to invite them in, and bid them to be seated. Everybody looked relieved, including Antoine. At first it seemed rather strange to be gathered under such unexpected circumstances, but Angel was glad that everything had finally come into the open, and she could at long last relax after the ordeal she had endured. Angelique was very touched that Alex had accompanied Grandma Lemoin, and they had brought along gifts for herself and the baby. It was like being a real family at long last, and she counted her blessings.

It turned out to be a superb afternoon for all; they made up for lost time, and finally dropped the subject, and concentrated on Angelique and the baby who was going to bring so much joy to the whole family. Eric later interrupted by suggesting that the mother to be needed to eat if she wanted a healthy baby, so he invited everyone to their favourite seafood restaurant Langoustin, because they had a lot to celebrate.

Eric brought Angelique home after they enjoyed a delicious meal and everybody else had left, including Antoine, who was invited to spend the weekend at his parents' place, as they hadn't seen him in months. Angelique thanked Eric for bringing her home, but he wasn't going to leave, so he invited himself in for a night cap and they chatted for old times' sake. Everything turned out to be natural and normal, and it was as though they had never been apart. Eric was having a hard time leaving Angelique on her own and asked her if he could stay the night. Angelique didn't mind at all, and Eric listened to the baby's heartbeat, and was thrilled when he kicked.

It was the rebirth of an enduring relationship, because very shortly thereafter Eric moved in with Angelique, and accompanied her to the last ultrasound before the baby's birth. It was Eric's first experience, he had never participated in something as extraordinary before. When Doctor Muller pointed out the baby's genitals, and made him listen to his heartbeat, Eric was the happiest man alive and couldn't wait for his son to come into the world, so that he could hold the bundle of joy in his arms. He was very proud indeed.

He had received a legal document in the post some days later informing him that he was a free man. He immediately proposed to Angelique, and had the ceremony organised in Marula at the castle, even though the elaborate reception would have to wait until after the child's birth. They had made arrangements for their wedding to take place on the 8th April, as the baby was due two weeks from then. Grandma Lemoin had organised everything, and the wedding was to take place at the castle as originally planned, only this time it wasn't going to be as elaborate, because Angelique was pregnant.

They planned to have a quiet family affair, and have a big reception immediately after the baby was born. Saturday morning on 8th April, Angelique and Eric got married at the court of justice, witnessed by Antoine and André, and then went over to the castle to celebrate. The arrangements were absolutely divine, everything was laid out with only the finest china and silver, and the company who catered for their meals was the best known caterer in the republic, Liegois Du Delice. They dined and danced all night long and had a lovely time, until the early hours of the morning, when Angelique's waters broke. She thought to herself that it could not have been a false alarm, so she told the others not to panic, while Grandma Lemoin called the doctor and an ambulance just in case she needed emergency treatment.

An hour later she started having labour pains, and real heavy contractions. The doctor was on his way. Grandma Lemoin had changed the blue room into a maternity ward, by sterilising everything she got hold of. On the other hand the men boiled water, Edwina made her daughter-in-law comfortable on an old stretcher which they had cleaned thoroughly, and threw over some spotless white sheets. Edwina was happy that she had found the stretcher because it was identical to the real thing required for childbirth.

When the doctor finally arrived, Angelique had already been in labour for two hours, and this carried on for another two. She was totally exhausted, but there was no time to rush her to the clinic, she was going to have a home delivery. Doctor Portnoir contacted Doctor Muller, and was given the go-ahead to do the delivery, but the baby seemed to be in no hurry. Finally, after almost three hours of hard labour, Angelo made his way into the world on 9th April at four in the morning, assisted by Eric, who had proudly cut the chord. The midwife held the child upside down, and beat his buttocks, until he gave a hungry cry, and all was well.

The doctor had to deal with the mother, and he was particularly concerned about why the afterbirth had not followed. He waited a few more seconds and then he started to panic. He accumulated all the medical instruments and forceps to scrape her immediately. Suddenly he saw another little body trying to make its way out, so he acted very cautiously and removed the baby with forceps because it was breach-positioned. Angelique was having a really hard time. She had endured so much pain and was praying for it to be over. She couldn't have an epidural for an unexpected delivery. Within no time a little girl came into the world to join her twin brother. The doctor felt that it would be advisable to get them into the clinic until they were out of danger. Just before they left, Grandma Lemoin got out a picture of her mum, when she was a baby. Grandma kissed the baby's fragile head, and mentioned that she would make a lovely Anemone. It was agreed upon that she be named Anemone, and there was no question about that.

After Angelique was discharged from the clinic, they called in an interior decorator, to do the twins' rooms, as all the preparations for Angelo had already been made and they had not anticipated having two children in one go. They lived in Angelique's house, while their dream home was being built in the upper class area of Calicorne, and the big wedding celebration was to take place shortly. Once again, they left it up to Grandma Lemoin to arrange things, and Angelique could finally get into her dream wedding gown and have the wedding of the year. They got married in St Theresa's Cathedral and had a fairy-tale wedding. They were unable to go on their honeymoon as planned because of the twins, and frankly they preferred to spend the time with their children.

The twins were going to celebrate their first birthday party when they moved into their superb double-storey mansion called 'Twin Pads' on the main boulevard. They chose a corner plot and created a massive garden area, where they could build a mini golf course and sports field for the kids. Angelique loved exotic trees and plants, and had palm trees planted around the swimming pool. In the back yard, they had massive servants' quarters and a big fish pond and a fountain with sculptured marine animals such as dolphins, barracudas and marlins. It was absolutely divine. They had installed one of the biggest swimming pools in the neighbourhood, and everything they built was out of the ordinary.

About a hundred metres from where they lived they had a neighbour, Mrs Verité who had two teenage sons, Jason and Keanan, rather strange boys. They had this thing about heavy metal and rock music that could perforate any eardrum. Their father had died and they turned out to be drug addicts. About a week after Angelique and Eric had settled in and could find their way around the area, they introduced themselves to the neighbours and familiarised themselves with the essentials they needed to know. They were very reserved, and knowing that their neighbour had problems, they stuck to their family orientation.

Arrangements were being made for the big celebration – they were to have a double party for the twins' first birthday and their wedding anniversary. They invited relatives and friends, so Angelique was always checking the postbox for replies, so she would know how many people to cater for, but this time the postman had a personal delivery from an anonymous sender, and the parcels were addressed to each child. It was a little bit in advance but Angelique immediately opened up the cute blue package, obviously for Angelo, and it contained a remote-controlled aeroplane, whereas Anemone's pink package contained a cuddly white teddy bear, much taller than she was herself. Angelique was disappointed at not knowing who sent the gifts, because she could not thank them, but she felt that it was a rather peculiar gift for a boy his age; she would keep it in the pantry until he was old enough to handle it.

When Angelo was two years old he was very intelligent and had a lot of constructive toys, so she gave him his aeroplane and showed him how to use the remote control. A few minutes later the plane had blown up in his tiny little face, leaving him slightly scarred, and he was in a state of shock and needed treatment. They later found out that the company who manufactured the toy was sued because of such accidents, but the specific toy was off the market, because it was discontinued the following day and all the existing models destroyed immediately thereafter. So no orders were sent out at all.

Angelo had healed and the plane incident had been forgotten. Angelique was enjoying motherhood. Anemone and Angelo were adorable, and her marriage to Eric couldn't be better. Eric's family treated her as their very own daughter, and she was totally fulfilled.

One day the postman came by, and she rushed out to get the post. She gathered up the envelopes and noticed a black one at the bottom of the pack and wondered what it contained. She had never seen a black envelope posted before. When she checked to see where it came from she realised that it had been put into the letter box, and hadn't been posted. The letter was addressed to Eric, so she waited until he got home. It turned out to be threatening notes, cut out of newspapers. They ignored the first few menaces, until it became life threatening, and they had it reported to the police, and their home was being watched. Since then the notes stopped and no one was caught, and life continued as usual. It wasn't really something they worried about. Thinking that it obviously came from Murielle, they ignored it.

Some time later, Eric had gone to work out at his gym club as he did three times a week. He did his exercises for an hour and went into the locker room to shower. The first cubicle was not vacant, so he went into the second. He heard a third man enter while he applied some gel douche to his skin. It sounded as if the door was being locked, but that was impossible because they were automatic doors, and needed to stay open for other gymnasts and guests coming from the swimming pool. He put it out of his mind and ran the water while his neighbour in the first cubicle sang a song called *He Ain't Heavy* that he would remember for the rest of his life.

Another gentleman occupied the third cubicle and within seconds Eric saw a cord flying above his head with a buzzing sound, but before he realised that it was an electrical appliance, it had already hit the floor in the first cubicle, electrocuting the young man and causing a sudden breakdown in the overall current.

Eric was completely panic-stricken, when he realised that it could have been him. By the time he got to the man the other had already disappeared from the third cubicle. The manager and other gymnasts hurried to see what had happened. Suddenly it occurred to Eric that he had been threatened some time back. The threatening notes he received were never death-threatening, but he had a feeling that this accident had been targeted at him. He needed to be extremely cautious in the future.

Things were really getting out of hand, the incidents and now death-threatening notes started multiplying, so they did some investigations. They warned Murielle, but she denied having anything to do with any of the incidents that had occurred. She couldn't understand how they could even suspect her of something so grotesque. Murielle started regretting having met a Lemoin in her life, and she cursed them for causing so much friction in her family. She especially hated Alex, because he had managed to send her father to jail, where he had been for more than a year now, and still had a great many years to serve.

Because of all the damages done and the large sum of money that couldn't be found, Luc Fourbourg's possessions were being taken away from him in order to repay his bills. Their cars were being repossessed and they were forced to move out of the home they had grown up in which they so cherished. It was very hard for Mrs Fourbourg who had spent so many years in her home, she loved entertaining and almost never did anything that wasn't domesticated. They were forced to sell their properties to make ends meet. They eventually moved out of their glamorous house in Calicorne, to a middle-class apartment in Rotanda, and Murielle felt terribly embarrassed. She had managed to keep the car her father had bought for her twenty-first birthday present and she could thank her lucky stars for that. Indra had moved in with her gorgeous boyfriend, Pedro, who refused to have anything to do with her family.

Since Luc had been jailed Mrs Fourbourg had been receiving an income from an anonymous person. A cash order voucher was being delivered to her letter box on a monthly basis. She didn't have a clue who it came from, but it permitted her to keep, up to a certain extent, the standard of living she was accustomed to. Murielle tried to bring about a reconciliation with Angelique, but Angelique couldn't forgive her for being false and she just wouldn't hear a word about it. Angelique had told Murielle that she could not erase all the years of their friendship, but it was very hard for her to accept Murielle after she had deliberately tried to entice Eric. It would have been different if she too were a victim, like Eric, but she had proved the contrary and it was a planned thing. She wouldn't trust her ever again, and being friends meant trusting and caring and she didn't have any left for Murielle.

Murielle didn't let her have the last word. Before leaving, she was so infuriated that she told Angelique what a plain Jane she was, and that she could thank her lucky stars that both Antoine and Eric felt the way they did towards her. Murielle told her that she was right, she never really considered her to be her best friend, but she did need to keep on good terms with her for Eric's sake, because she loved Eric and would have done anything to entice him, so she had better hold on to him for dear life, because the battle wasn't over. Murielle had made all kinds of threats towards Angelique before leaving.

A year had gone by since, and Antoine had gone back to travelling although he visited Calicorne as often as he could. The twins were now three years old and enrolled at the kindergarten. It was only about five hundred metres from where they lived so Angelique felt assured and close to them.

There was a private delivery once again, from the anonymous person they decided to name the invisible. Since their first birthdays they had been receiving presents in the post or by private delivery. This time, Angelo received a lovely puppy dog, a husky, while Anemone got a tiny white pony. Angelique was really taken aback and approved wholeheartedly the glamorous choice, but she still tried to find out who the expediter was. The people who delivered the animals were very vague and didn't have a clue who the person was. Firstly they were hired by telephone and given orders of what to do, and then they were paid in advance. All transactions were in cash and were placed into a safe at the international airport, so they left it at that.

A few months later, Angelo came from school and, as usual, he rushed to the back porch to greet Mozart, as he did everyday, and noticed that the dog was lying in a pool of blood. Angelo tried to revive his dog, but it was too late, he had been poisoned and strangled with a blue ribbon. Angelo cried bitterly and couldn't understand why someone would have wanted to take Mozart away from him in such a cruel way. Angelique had a hard time trying to get Angelo away from the dog's motionless body, but she eventually persuaded him away from the scene and then called the vet.

Recently they'd been having problems with their neighbour, Mrs Verité's sons were being very impolite, and used invectives all the time. Eric had warned them several times that if they didn't keep to themselves, he would have them locked up in a detoxification centre, where they would be forced to stay until they learnt some manners. The doctor had advised Eric and Angelique to get the same species of dog, so that Angelo wouldn't have time to think of Mozart's death. The very same afternoon they bought another husky, identical to Mozart, and named him Patches. People who didn't know about Mozart's death never noticed the difference, and called Patches Mozart. Angelo had finally forgotten about Mozart's death and really adored Patches, and Anemone sort of liked him too – they often argued about who the master was.

Scarcely five months later, they got home from a wedding to find Patches, poisoned and strangled, exactly the same way Mozart was, with a blue ribbon as well, and once again placed on the back porch. This time things had gone too far and Eric was a nervous wreck, worried about the children's safety. Eric had yet another quarrel with Jason, who threatened to shoot their dog if he came as close to his garden as he did. Eric was certain that they had killed the dog, and went over to Mrs Verité, for an explanation, but she told him to get off her premises before she called the cops. Eric went back home and called the police himself and got them to question her personally. Mrs Verité hadn't denied that her boys had a drug problem and that they were rude and often made threats, but they were kind-hearted boys and would never have carried out such threats, especially because they adored the twins, and they wouldn't do anything as sadistic. Eric had satisfied his curiosity and felt relieved, and for some reason or another he actually believed the woman.

On another occasion Angelo and Anemone had playtime at their nursery school playground, when a young lady, who had come to fill the vacancy as a tutor, organised some interesting games with the children on her day's trial. She especially took a liking to the twins. When they had played all the new games she had taught them, they were given a token of appreciation and a packet of sherbet in a red packet each, but because a king needed to be crowned the winner, she chose Angelo and handed him a golden packet of sherbet. The teacher told them that they were to eat their sherbet before they went home, and then brush their teeth thoroughly.

She had made a good impression on the principal of the nursery school, who told her that she was happy with the effect she had on the children, and that if she wanted the job she could start the following day. Later that evening Angelo kept on vomiting and had a fever. Angelique called the doctor who examined him. After the doctor had found out what they had eaten, he took them both over to the hospital to run some tests. Anemone was clear and as fit as a fiddle, while Angelo had certainly been poisoned, as the substance found in the bloodstream was extremely rare and lethal when taken in large quantities. They had been lucky that his body had rejected the poison and that it hadn't caused too much damage.

It took some time before they finally got some answers from the lab and had a warrant of arrest out for the lady, because it appeared that Angelo had been targeted and was poisoned. If Angelique hadn't brought Angelo to the hospital at that time, he would have ended up mentally handicapped or even brain-dead. The children's lives were in danger and the police had gone through the file of the lady in question and found that she was an immigrant from Poland in dire need of a job, and, like all applicants, she left a recent photograph of herself for the archives.

With the photograph given to them by the principal, the police managed to hunt her down for an explanation about the poisonous sherbet she had given Angelo. They arrived too late, someone else had already got to her before them, and shut her up for good. They had found her body behind a park bench in a nearby suburb. No witnesses came forward.

Minor incidents had occurred since then, but they managed to have a fulfilled life and carried on with their plans. It was already March when Angelique realised that they had been married for six years, and that the children would be six years old as well, so she got on the phone and asked Grandma Lemoin if she would come down to Calicorne to help out with some ideas for the party. They wanted to have a real big do.

As Indra was the only Fourbourg they actually got along with and she had become great buddies with Antoine, Angelique thought that it was a great idea to ask Indra to make the party frocks for at least thirty little girls and twenty boys. Indra was thrilled that Angelique had asked her to make the patterns, and she accepted with pleasure. She was a great stylist and assured Angelique that she would give it her best.

The Fourbourg family had just returned from the state prison in Baltimore, where their father had been serving for the past six years. It was never a pleasure to see how run-down he was, and he only had one thing in mind, and that was how to get vengeance. Indra had a heated argument with her father because of it. He continually tried to persuade her into getting important information regarding the businesses of the Lemoin family, and told her that he had been informed about the great relationship she was having with Antoine Lemoin, and he wanted her to get him to marry her.

Indra was shocked that her father could have sunk so low as to try to use her as a scapegoat, in exactly the same way as he did with Murielle. Indra was disgusted at her father's statement, and warned him that if he continued to make such suggestions, she would personally notify the Lemoin family that he was being unreasonable and making compromising suggestions, and she wouldn't hesitate cutting off all ties with them.

Murielle was even more disgusted with her sister for not agreeing with Luc, and a little jealous that Indra was having great success with Antoine and was even called upon to do the styling of the party frocks. She envied her sister and really wished that she had the privilege, but she would find other ways and means to rekindle the hearts of the Lemoin family somehow. An inmate had overheard the entire conversation, and carried it over to Antoine, who in turn informed the family. So they gathered that all the previous threats had naturally been coming from that angle, and that they would have a lead if anything else should occur or go wrong.

Angelique was pretty busy organising the playground and preparing her orders for the meals, as she was going to have two separate parties. The children's party would take place in the afternoon, while the adults were to spend the evening dining and dancing. A few days later, the family had a meeting, where they discussed important details that might have been left out, as they were catering for a large number of people. Antoine realised that the party was falling over the Easter weekend, so they could organise an Easter egg hunt for the children, and that would keep the men busy, painting hard-boiled eggs and hiding them all around the house. Angelique had ordered dozens of Easter eggs in all shapes and sizes, and had them delivered the morning of the party.

Finally, Saturday, 9th April arrived and the twins were very excited. Angelique and Indra had gone out at about ten o'clock in the morning to see the set-up in the garden where a Disney theme park had been installed, with their very own Mickey and Minnie, Donald Duck and so on. Angelique was very proud of the outcome and knew that the children were going to have the time of their lives. Both Eric and Antoine congratulated her on her outstanding achievement, and invited her to have a drink with them, while they looked at Indra's fairy-tale frocks in so many different colours.

Eric had asked Indra to stay for the children's party and participate in the dressing up. By twelve a dozen kids had arrived with their parents, and were making themselves comfortable with their playtime monitors who dressed them up in their party frocks, while their parents were offered drinks. Angelique had a few things to settle before the cameraman arrived to take some video pictures of the children's biggest birthday party yet, so she went into the lounge where Eric, Antoine, and Alex sat watching the end of the Formula One racing Grand Prix. She scolded them, telling them that they could be of much more help, when suddenly she noticed a clown walking towards the door, pushing a wheelbarrow. She burst out laughing when she saw the video man arrive behind the clown, pulling a trolley down the slash stone walk, and he seemed to have captured everything. This was going to be fun for the twins, so she sent the nursemaid to get them immediately.

The clown greeted the children by name and performed some of his acts, and wished them a happy birthday. He sang a song from a poem and then handed over their gifts and a card reading:

Happy birthday you two
from a rabbit named Who
who later died in the zoo, because he didn't make it to the loo
Take your time to gobble the bunny
until it makes a wobble in your tummy
A special chocolate for the both of you to chew.

They weren't interested in the clown and the song when they saw the massive Easter eggs on the trolley. They were wrapped up as a blue bunny rabbit and a pink bunny rabbit. The Easter eggs were just as tall as they were, so Angelique ordered Martha to take them up to the cooler and assured them that they would have permission to taste their rabbits on another occasion. Angelique said that they had too many luxuries, but they would eat some vegetables as well, so that they could taste a pretty bunny soon. Angelique knew that for the past six years they had been receiving outstanding presents from the invisible. She knew that sooner or later she would find out who this kind-hearted person was.

Much later in the afternoon, when the kids had eaten and played all their games, the parents were called upon to help the children open up their presents and tell them who they came from. Traditionally they generally started with Grandma Lemoin, who had offered Angelo a miniature electric motorbike. He could drive safely on the eighteen kilometre racing track for beginners. It was the real thing in miniature, and Angelo was very pleased indeed. He hugged Grandma tightly and kissed her cheek. Grandma Lemoin had offered Anemone a modern scooter in feminine colours, so she too could learn to drive at an early age. Angelo had got a set of junior fishing rods and the entire fishing kit, while Anemone got an aquarium with at least twenty different exotic fish. When all the other children had given out their presents, they finally ended with Eric and Angelique, who offered them both a portable television and video machine, so they didn't have to walk down a flight of stairs to see their favourite movies when they felt like it. Edwina and Luc invested in educational junior computers and constructive games.

Then there were the ones that were posted to them: one from Aunty Catherine in Australia, who had sent them T-shirts and shorts with kangaroos on them; and then another anonymous package, but this time it was no joke. In the blue package there was a black rose, with a card reading 'Gotcha now', while the pink package contained a pure white rose with a card reading 'Getcha later'. They decided to ignore the stupid joke and concluded the party to make way for the bigger celebration. All the other children were given lucky charms and packets on their way out and the party was a great success.

Later that evening the children had a light supper and were put to bed, while the adults enjoyed themselves. When the party was in full swing Angelique popped into the children's bedrooms to see if they were okay and not up to mischief. When she entered Angelo's room the kids were seated next to each other under the duvet watching *The Jungle Book*. Angelique smiled when she saw them and called Eric to have a look at the faces covered in chocolate. Angelique tucked Anemone into her own bed and told her to get some sleep, because they had to go to Sunday school the next day, and then they went downstairs to join the others. The party carried on up until the early hours of the morning, and they got to bed at about four thirty. The following morning they were awoken by Angelo.

'Mum, wake up, I have been trying to wake Anemone, but she doesn't want to get up, and we'll be late for Sunday school,' he said.

Angelique looked at her watch and realised that it was already ten o'clock in the morning, and it was rather unusual for Anemone to sleep that late. She got out of bed and pulled on her dressing-gown, when Angelo told her to hurry, because his sister was ill, and it looked as if she had fallen from the bed because her lips were blue. When Eric heard what Angelo had just said, he joined his wife and rushed up the staircase. Angelique shook her delicately trying to wake her up, but she wasn't responding, and then she noticed that her skin colour was different and her lips were rather greyish blue.

She had wrapped her daughter up in a bedspread and rushed to the car, while Eric alerted the emergency centre that they were bringing in an emergency. When they arrived, the medical staff worked rapidly, trying to save her life, and managed to pump her guts out to get rid of whatever was poisoning her system. The doctor was very worried and needed to know what she had eaten, they couldn't tell and didn't know exactly what could have caused it, but it was certainly not the party food, so it must have been something that an outsider had given her, and they would only find out when she regained consciousness. The doctors had run some tests and found that someone had intentionally wanted to kill the child, and it was certainly not with food.

Anemone lay helpless in the intensive care unit, where Deline had died exactly six years ago, and Angelique couldn't bear the thought of losing her daughter, so she prayed with all her might, while the other family members waited outside for some news. Hours had gone by and the doctors were still busy with Anemone, when finally the doctor came out and told them that she was out of danger, but she would need close monitoring because they had reason to believe that the child had been poisoned, or rather overdosed, by drugs. They had found a series of lethal drugs in her bloodstream, such as cocaine, heroine, LSD, pop, and other unidentified substances. The doctor also added that she was extremely lucky to have had a small dose, because only two more milligrams would have killed her.

After three days in the intensive care unit they finally got to ask Anemone what she had eaten, other than the food at the party. The other children tested for drugs had negative results and that meant that she was the only one to have had something different. Anemone was very weak and managed to remember, that she had eaten a lot of chocolate and marshmallows, and that Mrs Verité had given her a home-made caramel pop as she did on every birthday. She had also given one to Angelo, and it never made them sick before. Angelique told her to think carefully about a powdery substance that had a rather bitter taste, so Anemone remembered that she had eaten some Kool Aid, and she didn't know who it belonged to. She quite liked it and went back for more but the packet was taken away.

After their visit, Angelique and Eric called all the parents to find out which of their children had Kool Aid that day, but it appeared that half of the lucky packets contained Kool Aid. Kool Aid was a colourful powder one could make two litres of fruit drink from by adding water, and it came in different flavours. They later confronted Mrs Verité, without making accusations, and told her that they didn't appreciate her giving the children sweets without their permission. The police had followed every lead that sounded suspect, including Mrs Verité and her boys, who had a reputation for being nasty. They had previously been accused of killing the children's domestic animals, meaning that they were capable of anything, especially when they were under the influence of drugs.

After some enquiries a docket was opened for attempted murder and cruelty to animals, as well as disturbance of the peace. Anemone had to spend a month at the clinic and two weeks recuperating at home, and the police continued to investigate. They especially kept a close eye on Murielle and her family. When Anemone was ready to go back to school, her mum had already imprinted it into her mind that neither herself or her brother was to accept anything from strangers, and even if they knew the person, they should bring home whatever had been offered to them and ask for permission first.

Exactly a month later, Antoine came over for the weekend, as they had planned a camping and fishing trip with the whole family, and they had hired a combi deluxe to accommodate everybody. Angelique was happy when Antoine pulled up, as she could go into town to get fresh cold meats and salads and ice cold beers. Angelique asked Antoine to keep an eye on the children for a while. Antoine was only too glad to oblige because he wanted to show Angelo how to use his fishing rod, and they had a big fountain they could practice in.

Angelique had scarcely left when Angelo approached Antoine and threw one of his tantrums and asked Antoine if he could get his bunny rabbit out of the cooler. Antoine told him that his mum would be very angry, but that he was going to make an exception to the rule this time, and he could have his chocolate. Angelo hugged him and thanked him by telling him that his marshmallow Easter eggs were finished, and that someday or the other he would have to eat his bunny rabbit. Antoine agreed and helped him break off a piece of chocolate. Angelo was very generous. He had given Antoine a piece and offered

Anemone some as well, but Anemone was already busy finishing off a box of candy delight chocolates that Antoine had given to her when he arrived, and she enjoyed them all on her own.

Antoine wasn't in a chocolate mood, but he didn't want to offend Angelo and took a tiny little piece as well. It was a beautiful day, and the sun was shining – that made the chocolate melt. Antoine was wearing a white Lacoste sweater, completely smudged with Angelo's clumsy fingerprints.

When Angelique got back she laughed at the sight of her twins and their uncle, who somehow managed to be soaking wet with a video camera in his hands. Angelo was smudged in chocolate, all over his white safari suit, while Anemone was building sandcastles in a puddle of mud, and looked like a dirty doll, and she too was wearing white dungarees. It was quite a sight to see. She laughed, while Antoine just carried on getting the children to do some hilarious tricks, so that he could capture the funny parts. Antoine pretended to be filming Angelique, and managed to get hold of her and throw her into the fountain where the children jumped in after her. It was totally hilarious.

Everyone was having so much fun that they hardly noticed Eric's presence. Since his brother was in the mood to do a family movie, he decided to jump in, boots and all, followed by Mrs Lemoin and Alex, who turned up a while after. Grandma Lemoin was less courageous and didn't like getting all wet, so she walked over and dipped her feet into the water. Antoine pushed her in, but she held on to him and managed to get him into the water as well. It was a lovely afternoon, and they decided to have some fun. When they had finally showered and sat down for dinner, Eric thought that it was a great idea to see the video before the kids went off to bed.

It was really hilarious. They haven't had so much fun in a long time. This was the best that Antoine had achieved, out of all the family videos he had taken, and it would be of great sentimental value. The following morning, all the ice boxes were ready, and the combi was loaded. They were to have breakfast before leaving, so everyone sat down to eat and Anemone joined them, all ready for the trip. Eric had called Angelo three times already, so he decided to go up and hurry him along. Antoine followed him, saying that he wanted to go over the worm bit with Angelo.

When they got to Angelo's bedroom door, it was locked. Antoine banged a few times, but the child did not answer. Eric laughed, while he told Antoine why Angelo locked his door, believing that some burglar would come and steal his precious stamp collection.

After a minute or two Antoine thought that the child was fast asleep or playing a joke on them, but Eric knew differently. He had a premonition that something was radically wrong, so he broke down the door and walked towards his son's bedside, and realised that he was still asleep. Eric shook him, and told him that they were going on their first fishing trip together and that he had better hurry, joking that they would miss the big white shark. After a few seconds, he realised that history was repeating itself and he shook the child uncontrollably, while Antoine told him to be careful not to scare him.

Antoine touched the child's head and listened to his pulse and just looked at him once, and said, 'It's too late.'

Eric was hysterical, 'What do you mean too late? I don't care what time we get there, but Angelo has to wake up right now. We are big buddies, like all fathers and sons we are going fishing. Sometimes we'll go and play some golf and even go hunting if he wants to.'

Eric continued blabbering about all the things he wanted to do with his son, while the tears streamed down his face.

Antoine was in a state of shock and tried to get Eric away from Angelo, but he wouldn't let go of Angelo's hand.

'He told me how much he loved me last night, and asked if I wouldn't change my mind about taking him hunting one day, and, strangely enough, I told him that we would start by fishing and that we would do anything else he wanted us to. Thank God I let him believe that he had my permission to do the impossible, but I didn't tell him to die.'

With all the commotion coming from upstairs, Angelique thought that Antoine and Eric were arguing about something, and reminded them that there was no time for childishness, everyone was ready to leave. When no one responded, she decided to go and calm them down. She walked into the room, and immediately knew that her son was no longer of this world. She rushed over and looked at him; he looked as if he was just asleep, but she knew that he had passed away. She passed out.

Downstairs Mrs Verité rang the doorbell and found the front door ajar. There was nobody in sight, so she rang again and decided to push the door, when she overheard screams from upstairs. She did not hesitate to run up the staircase to see what had happened. When she finally got to the bedroom she realised that something grave had happened, she looked at Angelo and saw that he was slightly blue, and that his feet were cold. Mrs Verité covered his face with the sheet, and ordered Antoine to call the undertakers, a doctor and an ambulance, as well as the police. Eric had been trying to revive his wife but to no avail, and they both stood over her like zombies. Mrs Verité removed the eucalyptus from the medicine chest and asked for a handkerchief, and then rubbed the oil across Angelique's nostrils until she recovered. Angelique finally came to, but seemed to have lost her memory.

By now the others were back from the garage, where they had filled the petrol tank and bought some refreshments for the road and were all ready to leave. Alex felt that something happened, and he went into the bedroom, followed by Anemone, who became hysterical when she saw her brother's face covered with a sheet. She pulled it off, and kissed him, and told him that she couldn't go camping without him, and would stay at his bedside until he got better. Mrs Verité managed to pull her away from him. It was the most tragic day in the lives of everyone present.

The coroner had come and certified Angelo dead on arrival, and got his body taken to the mortuary, where they needed to carry out an autopsy. About ten minutes later the police had arrived to take down statements, when Angelique suddenly came to her senses. She realised what had happened and looked at Mrs Verité. Angelique reacted unexpectedly. She took a crystal vase and swung it directly at Mrs Verité and accused her of killing her son.

'You tried to kill my daughter, now you've succeeded in killing my son, why? What have I done to you?' she said. 'Just what have I done other than help you?'

The vase had struck Mrs Verité and she was being attended to by the doctor, who had given her some stitches in her head.

The detective insisted on knowing why Angelique made accusations concerning Mrs Verité, Angelique explained that Mrs Verité and her sons were suspects in the recent events. So they took down her version of the story and asked her not to leave the area as they would need her for questioning. Mrs Verité told them that she had no reason to leave town and that she was very hurt by the accusations made by Angelique. Mrs Verité told them how Angelo used to phone her and put in his order for caramel pops, and he would come and get them when his mum was out of sight.

She had been making caramel for them since their second birthday she said, and cried hysterically. Grandma Lemoin gave her a sedative and offered to make tea for everyone.

Angelique and Eric were totally drained after Angelo's body was taken away and the police had finally left too. Mrs Verité could not bring herself to leave, so they sat there thinking of what could have happened. Then Angelique realised that the evening she found Anemone all chocolatey, she had been poisoned, and just yesterday Angelo ate nothing else but chocolate, because they didn't have any other chocolates except their bunny rabbits. She asked Antoine which chocolates they ate. Antoine told her that he had brought a box of choco deluxe which they were to share between them, but Angelo wanted to taste his bunny rabbit instead.

She suddenly got to her feet and said out aloud, 'Why in God's name didn't I think of the chocolate, yes the chocolate?'

Angelique ran up to the cooler box and opened it up. She stood there, looking at the evidence. Anemones Easter egg was still intact, while Angelo's had been eaten. She asked Anemone if she had also eaten Angelo's Easter egg, before she got sick. Anemone told her that she was sorry that she broke a piece of Angelo's chocolate, but he could have half of hers to replace the piece she had eaten.

Now there was absolutely no doubt whatsoever that the famous Easter eggs were the cause of her son's death. She took both chocolates to the laboratory where they were tested. Mrs Verité, asked no questions and just followed Angelique wherever she went, without saying a word. It felt so right that she be with this family in their time of need. Later that afternoon they were waiting for a call from the lab, and had a couple of drinks. Eric drowned his sorrows in doubles of whisky, while Antoine tried to pacify him. The ladies kept each other company and Mrs Verité had not left Angelique's home since the early morning. Angelique realised that she had cast false accusations, and apologised. Mrs Verité told her that she understood. It must have been a double surprise to see her on the premises she had never set foot on in five years, but she had a serious problem and she didn't know who to turn to, besides Angelique. She told her that she was paying for the boys' detoxification, and she had run short and wanted to borrow some money for food. Mrs Verité told Angelique that she had no alternative but to put her pride aside and ask for some food or money to buy some, as she hadn't eaten for two days. Angelique felt very bad and they all wept then. It was pathetic to live under such circumstances. Mrs Lemoin got the cook to prepare a meal with all the food they had intended to take to the picnic, so that Mrs Verité could get something immediately.

After an autopsy had been done on Angelo, they had made some comparisons with Anemone's food poisoning results, and found that the contents of the chocolate in Angelo's bloodstream were exactly the same as those found in Anemone's previously, and that they came from only one chocolate, that which had belonged to Angelo.

Anemone's Easter egg was clear and it was evident that the person who sent it wanted Angelo dead, and didn't mean for Anemone to get hold of her brother's chocolate, that is why it was specifically wrapped in blue. Everything coincided with the blue ribbon strangling of the dogs, the black rose, an aeroplane that blew up in his face. A docket of first degree murder was opened up and they thought that all the crimes were certainly committed by someone who hated the Lemoin family. Antoine also needed to undergo tests, because had eaten some of Angelo's chocolate and needed to be treated.

Investigations were carried out around the chocolate factories in the area it couldn't be very difficult to find the manufacturer of the specific style, as there were only two such factories, and they manufactured different types of chocolate, so they managed to pin down the factory where such settings were used. It happened to be the well-known Candairies Chocolux factory. They were to find out who had been dealing with that specific batch of Easter eggs, and who had moulded, set and wrapped them. They found out that ten casuals were hired over the Easter period and that five of them worked on that batch. All the names and addresses of the casuals were given to the inspector, and among the names was that of Fabrice Fourbourg.

The inspector thought that he had found his man, and was very excited, going directly to the gentleman's apartment to question him. Fabrice didn't have a clue about what they were insinuating, until they reminded him that he was related to Murielle Fourbourg, who happened to be a prime suspect. They had advised him to tell the truth, but they were absolutely wrong, because Fabrice did paperwork for the orders and never laid hands on a single chocolate, and he wouldn't even for the sake of the Fourbourg name.

It was not as easy as they thought it would be. When they had gone through the eighth person they finally got a clue. They spoke to Albert Kock, who happened to work on the same batch that day. He told them that Fakhir Ramdam asked him to keep some of his rejects for him to remelt before he left that day. He mentioned that he was going to remelt them for two Easter eggs for his twin cousins.

'We were not earning a fantastic salary, so I asked Janeiro to keep some of his rejects as well, and Fakhir paid us, which was abnormal because we were allowed to take packets of broken chocolates without any trouble.'

The inspectors went over to see Fakhir. He welcomed them in and asked them to be seated. He didn't deny or argue about having made the Easter eggs, and explained to them that a young lady had come to him, while he was on his lunch break, which he often spent sitting under a tree reading a book. She walked up to him and asked him if he could do her a special favour, and gave him a bundle of notes. He told the inspector that he hadn't seen so much money in a long time and thought that it would do no harm to listen to her proposition, and it was rather straightforward. She told him that she had twins and that they both suffered from cholera. She had been looking for a way to get her son to take his dose of medicine, but he just wouldn't. She told him that the little girl, had no problem with taking hers.

'She said that the little boy was a chocoholic. She even told me his name was Angelo and that he was very naughty, and the only way to get him to have his intake was to get him to eat something that he liked without knowing that it contained his medicine. She had given me a bottle of powder, and even gave me the prescription to read. You see, there was no reason for me to doubt the woman. Everything she requested seemed harmless, and she paid me enough for it, she told me not to put anything into Anemone's Easter egg.'

At long last the police were making headway, but there were a lot of questions left unanswered. For instance, they needed to know who had got in contact with the clown, and find out his identity, and whether he knew that he was delivering a lethal chocolate. Fakhir informed them that he immediately told Janeiro about what the lady wanted him to do, and he was aware of the powdery substance that was put into the chocolate. Fakhir told them that he had asked Janeiro to do the delivery, and the woman had even paid for the clown's outfit.

'You must realise that when she initially asked me to do the chocolates, she had already given me quite a bit of cash. At that time it didn't sound excessive and it was a fast buck. It seemed relatively easy. I paid Janeiro to deliver the Easter eggs at the address she gave me. She was very specific that they were going to have a big party that day; she even gave me a card with a poem or something that Janeiro was to sing. She left a considerable amount of money in a safe at the airport and left the key in a locket with the password and we got our money.'

Fakhir was asked if he could identify the lady in question and act as a witness in court. After having heard about Angelo's death, Fakhir didn't hesitate for one second, and told them that he felt guilty and would do anything to get justice done, and that the least he could do was to identify the woman.

The following week they had a parade of six different women, and Fakhir was asked to point out the woman who was responsible for Angelo's death. Without hesitation he pointed to Murielle, and she was asked to leave the room under surveillance. The police thanked Fakhir, and told him that he was not to leave the country, and that they would get in contact with him if they needed to. Murielle was arrested for culpable homicide with aggravating circumstances and was refused bail. She was furious. She insisted that she didn't have a clue as to why she was being arrested. The inspector informed her and read her rights to her and had her taken to a cell for the evening, until they could transfer her to another county jail.

Murielle appeared in court, and pleaded not guilty to all counts and told them that she had been framed, but she did not convince the jury and was sentenced to ten years' imprisonment of which she had a suspended sentence for six years because of the lack of proof. She spent exactly two years in prison. Murielle was behind bars in the same prison as her father, who had now been in prison for eight years. Indra couldn't understand why Murielle did something so cruel to an innocent child, and she wanted to understand, but Murielle remained adamant that she had absolutely nothing to do with any of the crimes.

Murielle had anticipated getting out after she had served two years in prison, but things were being prolonged. She knew that she wouldn't do much more than three, but she dreamed about getting back to civilisation. Her father still had a few more years to do before he got out.

For the Lemoin family everything got back to normal. They hadn't received any other threatening notes, and there were no other incidents, since Murielle was behind bars. Angelique had finally come to terms with Angelo's death, but Eric suffered a great deal, although he managed to part with all Angelo's personal belongings in order to forget. Some time later, they had a phone call from Luther asking them to come over to the castle immediately, because Grandma Lemoin had passed away. Angelique was very delicate about how she broke the news to Eric and Antoine so she wouldn't traumatise them.

Alex and Edwina had already been informed and arrived at their home, ready to leave immediately. They had arrived a couple of hours later and everything was arranged as she had requested in her will: that she be buried the very next day after her death, and that the will be read immediately thereafter. She had suffered a stroke, and died instantly.

The funeral was held at the castle, and she was buried at the castle's graveyard, as she called it, because all her ancestors were buried there, as requested in her last will and testament. After the burial, everybody gathered at the castle and assembled in Grandma Lemoin's favourite lounge, where, at her request, a video was being shown with a message for everyone. When everyone was ready, Attorney Griffiths ran the video, and asked everyone to listen attentively.

'Hi everybody, no more tears, when you all see this, I'll be someplace else looking down on all you wonderful people who have made my life worthwhile. I have shared so many joyful moments with all of you in this castle and now I am no longer. So I'd like all of you to have something, so that my memory can live on, as did my forefathers.

'To start off with, to my eldest grandson and his wife, Angelique, and their children, I leave the castle with all its contents, as well as the vineyards and the winery. Three apartment buildings, Clarendon Heights, Balmoral Residential Suites and Palm Beach Holiday Resort, a partnership between Eric and Antoine for E & A enterprises.

'I demand that all the staff members of the castle be held on in family service, and be duly rewarded for their loyalty. A bank account had been opened for each of my great-grandchildren Anemone, Angelo the second, Leandra and Leonardo... you might think that I am crazy, but I know that you will be having other children shortly, and I have a feeling that they will be making their way into the world in the very near future.

'To my grandson, Antoine, I leave three apartment buildings, and Mountain's Peak resort as well as a percentage of the winery's income and a partnership in E & A enterprises. A bank account has been opened in your name, and another for your future children.

'I take it that I have had my final say, as you all know I always have the last word. I wish you all every success, and hope that you will have a long and happy life in Marula, and welcome you to your new abode.'

Eric was overwhelmed by the thought of being the owner of the superb Castle of Marula, and was very honoured to have inherited all its contents, including the winery. Antoine was very happy too, and he joked about the fact that Grandma Lemoin was very generous, but that she had forgotten to give him even one room in the castle he adored so much.

Eric looked at him, quite surprised at his remark, and understood that the castle meant a lot to him. He said, 'For God's sake, Antoine, you know that this is your home just as much as it is ours, this castle is and always has been a family affair and will stay that way for many more generations to come, and it will always belong to the entire family.'

When everything was over they hugged and returned to their respective homes in Calicorne.

There were going to be big changes in their lives and they needed to make arrangements for their move to Marula. They most certainly had to wait for Anemone to finish off her school year, and then hire out Twin Pads in Calicorne. They adored their home but were quite happy to start somewhere else far from all the morbid things that had happened at their house, but there was no way they were going to sell their dream home.

Mr and Mrs Lemoin felt sad that they weren't going to see as much as they would have liked to of Eric and Angelique, meaning that they would have to drive up to Marula occasionally to see them, but for the meantime they would make the most of it while they were still in Calicorne. Things were taking shape back at Marula, where the constructors were well underway with the new ultra-modern golf course that was nearing termination. They had also planned on refurbishing the existing swimming pool, but, because of the old stone, they needed to keep it in the original style, so they lengthened the deep end and turned it into an Olympic pool.

They were not quite ready to move to Marula, not for at least five more months, that was when Anemone would have finished her school term. Angelique hadn't been feeling well recently, so she asked her mother-in-law to accompany her to see Doctor Muller. He announced that she was pregnant, and anaemic, and that he preferred her to take it easy for the next few months, with an antenatal visit once a month. Angelique was thrilled. She told Eric about it, and he praised the Lord for small mercies. He hoped that they were going to have a boy this time, no doubt to replace Angelo, and Angelique hoped so too, for his sake. Everybody else was happy as well, and Antoine was totally thrilled when he heard the news.

Mrs Lemoin was proud to have been of some help during the first months of Angelique's pregnancy, but it was quite difficult, because she suffered morning sickness and felt tired all the time. She couldn't stand going to a restaurant, because she always ended up being nauseous, so Mrs Lemoin drew up her menu for the cook and ensured that she did not get too many rich dishes and had lots of vegetables. Eric was absolutely thrilled himself to take part in the antenatal classes, and wanted to make up for not having taken part in the first pregnancy.

Anemone had just celebrated her ninth birthday, and was ready to conquer a whole new way of life; she was going to have a new brother and sister in a short while, as they had found out that Angelique was expecting twins. One weekend the whole family decided to drive up to the castle and spend a few days there, in order to make the final arrangements for the big move. Angelique had planned to have the twins at the Monté Carlin Clinic in Calicorne, because she was already seven months pregnant, and Doctor Muller had been treating her all the time. She didn't feel like having another doctor do the delivery.

They had arrived early afternoon on the Friday, and had time to inspect the work that had been carried out. It was beautiful, the golf course had eighteen holes, and was arranged in such a way that it had little dams of water, with fountains and bridges to get to the other side; the bunkers were superb, looking like sand dunes from a distance; it was really outstanding. The garden had been turned into an island with exotic trees and plants all over the place, but they had not removed the existing trees and plants. As for the swimming pool, it was divine, and finally the fishpond was exactly the same, but slightly refurbished, and a whole school of fish now lived there and it was being properly maintained.

Everybody had a shower and settled in. While Eric, Antoine and Alex went for a round of golf, the girls decided to have a swim instead. Later, the evening dinner was being served, and everyone was present when Angelique suddenly felt something running down her legs. At first she thought that she was imagining things, but when she put her hand on her leg to feel, she knew that her waters had broken, and she didn't want to alarm anyone just yet. Angelique knew that she had to get to a hospital as quick as possible, because she was not due. She waited for the right moment to tell everybody that the twins were on the way, and that she wouldn't make it to the hospital on time, because she had unbearable labour pains.

Edwina got on the phone and called Doctor Portnoir, who promised to be there within the next ten minutes. Angelique was very worried about the twins, she hoped that they would survive. Doctor Portnoir arrived and told them that he had a feeling that the night was going to be interesting, while he examined Angelique. He remembered delivering Angelo and Anemone under the same circumstances, but he didn't know that Angelo had passed away. The doctor wasted no more time and got to work. The first baby was no trouble at all, he rushed out without the slightest problem. Angelo the second arrived, followed by Leandra, his little sister. She had scarcely popped out her head when another little being made his way into the world totally unexpectedly. Leonardo cried immediately as he made his appearance.

It was phenomenal that she had twins, when she was supposed to have only one, and had triplets when she was supposed to have twins. Angelique was grateful that everything went off well, and she hadn't suffered too much. They were rushed to the Marula clinic, situated at least thirty minutes away. When they arrived at the clinic the triplets were put into incubators, and their mum was being held under observation. Angelique underwent a general check-up and asked the doctor to sterilise her temporarily, because she couldn't understand why she was having multiple births. The doctor told her that it probably had a lot to do with the fact that she had been on fertility drugs for so many years, and now she was recompensed with a gift from God.

Eric was like an excited child as he posed for the reporter holding up his triplets and was as proud as a peacock. The triplets were tiny and fragile and could fit into shoeboxes, it was amazing how small their hands and feet were. Anemone said they looked like little dolls and she was very proud indeed. Angelique had stayed at the clinic for over a week and breastfed the babies, who were now out of danger. She was discharged from the clinic and went home, leaving the triplets to put on more weight before they finally got to come home, with the result that she did three feeds a day and the midwives did the rest.

Angelique went home to get a decent meal, because Edwina had prepared the meal especially for her. Edwina knew that Angelique could not stand rich food during her pregnancy, so she prepared only the best and it turned out to be delicious. They were having freshly baked apple strudel and hot custard for dessert, when the telephone rang.

'Can I speak to Mrs Lemoin please?'

'Speaking,' she said.

'Madam, this is the superintendent of the Marula clinic, I'm afraid that something has happened and your presence is required as soon as possible.'

'What are you talking about, are my babies ill?'

'No, they've been abducted from the clinic.'

Angelique was hysterical, she kept repeating that they had kidnapped the triplets. When they arrived at the clinic Nurses Demos and Ross were in a state of shock, and seemed to be really sorry, but sorry wasn't going to bring back the triplets, so they needed an explanation, and pronto. Nurse Demos explained that after nine o'clock in the evening they had finished their feeds and retired to their office to do some administrative work, when a nursing sister walked in through the nursery as if she knew exactly where she was going, and as the office adjoined the nursery, there was no problem with that because she was staff.

The nursing sister introduced herself as Roumaine del Ponti, and told them that she was to get a prescription from the hospital's dispensary on the third floor, but she couldn't find it and it was rather urgent because she needed catheters and urological bags, for a patient who was going into surgery within an hour. She worked in the urology block on the fifth floor. There was no doubt that the prescription she held in her hand was from urology block five, and the patient happened to be someone Nurse Demos knew, because she read the prescription.

Nurse Demos told her that she was on the right floor, but she needed to go on to the west side of the corridor. She thanked them and turned around to leave, and sneezed, so she excused herself and put her hand into her pocket and pulled out a handkerchief, and suddenly sprayed a type of gas into the air and rushed out. Nurse Demos tried to get up from her seat but felt wobbly and then passed out and she had locked the door behind them.

Nurse del Ponti knew that they would be unconscious for at least ten to fifteen minutes, so she got to work immediately. The third floor was deserted, and there were about fifteen infants in the nursery, so she got hold of the laundry trolley and wrapped the triplets into some sheets and placed them into the trolley, assuring that they had enough air, but before that she had given them some nasal drops that would keep them sleeping for a few minutes until they were out of sight. She pushed the trolley down the corridor, trying not to attract attention, when she noticed a mum coming down the hall, but it would take her at least three more minutes to get to the nursery to see her baby, so she pressed the elevator button and it opened immediately, but a gentleman came from nowhere and joined her. He tried to make conversation and all she needed was to get rid of the man. She politely asked him why he was up at this time of the night. He told her that he couldn't sleep so he had decided to walk around. She suggested that he go back to the third floor and go to the all-night cafeteria and ask them to prepare a hot mint-flavoured tea and he would have a good night's sleep.

Miss del Ponti had arrived in the basement and got out of the elevator in a very normal manner, but she needed to rush because the lady she saw must have reached the nursery by then. The man thanked her and went back up, while she wheeled the trolley to the end of the basement floor and removed the children and placed them in a big basket which she had left at the entrance between the parking lot and the basement. She placed the triplets in the back of the car and drove to the security stop and greeted the security officer with a big smile. He asked her to sign the register and show him her identification card, so she did just that, and he smiled and let her go.

When she was out of sight she sped off because she was certain that already a hell of a commotion was going on back at the clinic. She laughed at the fact that the security officer didn't even notice that the card she handed to him was false and stolen, so he wasn't doing a thorough job, and because of that he was going to lose his employment, as they were very strict at the clinic.

Back at the clinic the police had arrived and sent some of their guys out to find a young lady in her early thirties driving a red Citi Golf registration number 0007 bang. At first the guys thought that they were joking, but it was true that it was the number plate on the car. They were replaying the video from the hidden camera, and distinctly saw the lady, and managed to get an identikit of her, but they didn't have any other leads, except for the Fourbourg family, so they phoned the traffic department, who didn't know who the car belonged to, because they had no such identification plates. They called all the car rental places and finally got a clue, amazingly about thirty of the exact same models had been rented out the same day, but only one female driver, all the others were men.

She had obviously changed the number plate so that she couldn't be identified straightaway. Right through the night they lived a nightmare; for all they knew, the woman could have exchanged vehicles and be well on her way out of Marula, but they had alerted the police department of Calicorne and they too were on the look out for such a car. At about midnight they had found the car abandoned on a deserted road leading off in various different directions, and it was very difficult to distinguish where she was heading.

The Calicorne police had followed all leads possible and searched all the Fourbourgs' homes and some of their friends' as well, but they found absolutely nothing, and Indra was outraged at the thought. She was sympathetic about what happened, but Murielle was in jail and they were still pursuing her. The detective, de Vito, agreed with her, and called off the search from the Fourbourgs' point of view.

The detective called to tell them about their findings and that they were looking in different circles altogether. Eric didn't care what Indra had to say, they needed to find his children. Antoine told them that they were to follow all leads no matter what, including Indra's boyfriend and Murielle's. He asked them if they had bothered to look at Pedro's or Paolo's villa. The detective told Eric that they had checked Pedro's and he had threatened to have them arrested for disturbing the peace and that Paolo was out of town.

Antoine was totally frustrated and told them so. They weren't doing their work, they had a search warrant and they could look anywhere they wanted to. Detective de Vito told them that he would send out the guys as soon as possible. Within an half an hour they had found Mrs Eldron at Paolo's villa in Manhaven and everything seemed to have been finely planned.

Mrs Eldron was set up in an underground type of storeroom, turned into a nursery for the triplets. Everything was neatly organised and a heater had been installed because it was pretty chilly down there. There were Milton's sterilising liquids for each child and it turned out that Mrs Eldron was a qualified nurse. There was only one way anyone could know where the secret room was, and that was by knowing where the trapdoor was. It was extremely difficult, because the marble tile design was exactly in line with the rest of the floor, so it looked like a normal tiled floor. If it wasn't for the carpet rolled untidily to one side they would never have found it.

The triplets were safe and sound and taken to the Monté Carlin clinic in Calicorne and examined. While their parents were heading for Calicorne, Mrs Eldron was being questioned. She admitted to having kidnapped the triplets, but she refused to name the person who hired her to do so. They negotiated with her that if she gave the name of the person, no charges would be pressed against her from the Lemoin family and she would get away with a fine and no imprisonment, or she could keep the silence and do ten more years behind bars, where she had just been for fraud. After a lot of thought Mrs Eldron decided to come out with the truth, but she felt guilty about taking the woman's money and having to tell on her.

Mrs Eldron finally admitted that she had been in Baltimore state prison for three years for fraud, because she had embezzled cheques to make ends meet, and she ended up paying behind bars. Then she met Murielle Fourbourg, who explained to her that her father was in the same prison, because of their ex-colleague and friend. She remembered that Miss Loni, who had married since and become Mrs Eldron, didn't like Angelique, and always complained that she was self-pitying, and terribly artificial. At first it felt quite strange, remembering how they got to know one another.

They had all worked at the Calicorne clinic, where Murielle and Angelique started straight after graduation and Mrs Eldron joined them about a year later. They had become friends, and spent a lot of time together. Murielle later left and Mrs Eldron went overseas to further her studies as a doctor, and met a man whom she fell in love with, who was studying medicine too. Mrs Eldron wasn't rich, but her parents paid for everything, including her living and studies. Peter was the ideal person for her: he was handsome, charming and stinking rich and he spoiled her, showering her with gifts.

After a few months she moved into a smart house, and he allowed her to choose out only the best furniture. He had even got her to sign documents of the house at the bank and at furniture stores. He told her that it was important, because he trusted her and wanted to make her his beneficiary one day, so she didn't even give it thought and signed any document. There was no reason why she shouldn't trust him; after all, he had so much money and he drove an expensive Porsche.

Peter maintained Miss Loni and he eventually persuaded her to quit studying for a while and try to have a baby, and continuing work after the child's birth. Miss Loni did anything Peter asked her to do, she was completely under his charms. Her parents had warned her that Peter was a gold-digger and that she was wrong to have left her studies to have a baby. After a year she still hadn't conceived, but it was already too late. When she got back from the doctor, Peter had left, and she walked into an empty home. He had only left her clothing, and not even a bed. She found a prescription that the doctor had given him, and she found out that he was a sufferer of AIDS. She panicked and returned to see the doctor who took tests, but she needed to wait for the results.

The first set of results were negative, so she needed to do a series of tests before she could be cleared of the virus. She later found out that the so-called Peter had somehow got hold of her family's bank account numbers and had managed to get away with a fortune. One day her parents went on holiday for two months, and Peter had arranged to have all their private belongings stolen and had emptied their bank accounts with false signatures and bank transfers. He had laid hands on her personal savings account, the money she had managed to save since he was supporting her, and had drawn out every dime, leaving her with only the clothes on her back.

The house they lived in belonged to both of them, because she had signed the buyers' act, and Peter had paid the first few instalments and left her with the arrears. The bank had been threatening to auction the house and drag them to court if they didn't pay up to date, but Miss Loni was not aware that he had taken out a bank loan, and it was by pure coincidence that she found the statements and warnings, with many more creditors. She was ashamed of herself for being so naive, but she needed to do something to repair the damage.

She was relieved when she remembered that her secret code bank account contained a considerable amount of money and she could pay off the house and her debt and then sell the house, so she went to her steel safe, and noticed that it was still intact. There was no way he could have got into the safe without breaking it, because it had a special key and a special code only she knew, and that was at her bank, so she went right over, removed the keys and the code book and returned home and opened up the box, only to find a ton of bricks in the safe. She was furious and in serious trouble, and couldn't understand how he could have broken into her safe at the bank, but then she remembered that he had managed to wipe out her parents' account, and that he was professional.

Miss Loni was forced to sign the house back to the bank and had her car repossessed. She was later turned away by her family because of the predicament she had put them in, and even if they wanted to help her they couldn't. They at least managed to keep their home and their car and some policy money. They were later paid out by the insurance company for the loss of their furniture, and were glad that they actually thought of insuring their property, unlike their hard-headed daughter who had cost them a lifetime of hard-earned money and sweat. They had warned her about the man several times, but she wouldn't listen. Peter had politely disappeared from the face of the earth, and never surfaced thereafter. Miss Loni didn't even know his real name at the time.

She was desperate, and needed to find a job as soon as possible, in order to repay all the debt she was held liable for. She had tried to worm herself out of the predicament, but her signature proved that she had agreed to the clauses in black and white and she had no excuses. The poor woman was unable to pursue her studies. Luckily she still had her nursing qualifications and experience and found a job at a general hospital, where she worked for years paying off a stranger's debt, and realised that she had only paid off the interest and still had the entire sum to pay off. She knew that if she didn't find a miracle to get herself out of the mess, she would work for the rest of her life paying off the debt.

Finally she got tired of working for a measly salary, so she started prostituting herself in her spare time, and met a very rich client who fell in love with her and would have done anything for her, but she didn't love the man and only had one idea – to get enough money out of him and leave. Mr Eldron asked her to marry him, and stop working as a call-girl. She was afraid of admitting that she had a mountain of debt, because he would have known that she was into the relationship only until her debt was paid up.

She started to steal cash from his home safe, and forged his signature to pay the accounts, and then he opened up a bank account under her name so she could use his money freely, and she managed to pay back every cent of debt and was a free woman. But she had become accustomed to Mr Eldron's riches, and spoilt herself. He permitted her to buy anything her heart desired, until he had a heart attack and died, leaving her his entire estate; and just to think that she wanted to get divorced from him. But later she was accused of killing her husband for his fortune, and that the testament would be blocked until she was proven not guilty. All her old debt was mentioned in court and even the forged cheques she had signed when Mr Eldron was alive. Then someone came along and told the police that Mrs Eldron had paid him to kill her husband and had given him a cheque for one million dollars, but that he refused and she told him that she would find someone else or do it herself.

Mrs Eldron found herself in exactly the same predicament she was some years back and thought to hell with it. She did inherit her husband's fortune but it was blocked, so she would apply for the company assets, but they too had been frozen until the entire estate was rounded up, and for the time being she needed a lawyer to present her in court. While the case was going through the motions, she had continued to use his credit cards and had stolen his son's cheque book and fraudulently signed false cheques adding up to almost two million. But this time she got caught in the act, and was arrested immediately.

She later found out that her stepson was the one who had contested the will. She had stayed in jail for the fraud, but she didn't know that recently she had been named sole executor of the entire Eldron estate and needed to pay back two point five million to his son and one million in damages, but she was rich enough to triple the amount and still live happily ever after.

She explained that she had worked all her life to repay another man's debt and had got tired of living that way. She was rather fortunate that she was not held liable for the amount of money after her release. But she didn't have a home to go to, so Miss Fourbourg offered her a huge amount of money in cash and asked her to kidnap the triplets from the Marula clinic.

Mrs Eldron apologised, and explained that she only did it for the money and that she would never have harmed the children, because Murielle promised that someone would come and get them the next day and that she would be free to go. 'If I had known that I had inherited my husband's estate, I would have told the lady to bugger off, but I was desperate,' she said.

Murielle denied every accusation against her and vowed that she had nothing to do with the scheme and that she had been set up once again. She told them that she had never committed a crime against the Lemoin family and pleaded her innocence. She did not deny that she had befriended Mrs Eldron since Calicorne clinic and met her again when they were cell-mates in Baltimore, and that they got along quite well. That was why she was having a hard time trying to understand why she was being framed.

Now that the children were safe and sound, they moved into the castle. Anemone had started her new school and seemed to be very happy and made lots of new friends. Anemone had turned out to be a real chatterbox and was a pretty little girl, while her little sister, who was only a year old, got a lot of her attention, because Angelo and Leonardo were two wild little ones and she couldn't keep up with them.

Angelique had created a women's club for the ladies in her neighbourhood and held meetings at least three times a week. Edwina and Alex came over every weekend and sometimes stayed a bit longer. Angelique had become friends with Melany, a really sweet girl, whose husband got on well with Eric. They often played golf together, and Barry was a real gourmet; he loved fresh cream pastries, so Eric got into the same habits and needed a lot of exercise because of his new hobby.

When the triplets were celebrating their third birthday, Anemone was twelve years old and turning out to be a beautiful young lady already. She was well built and looked very mature for her age; she was a bright student, a well-mannered girl and everyone adored her. Antoine was very fond of his niece and went out of his way to spoil all of them. He loved the boys and always bought toys and sweets for them. He loaded them with presents, but his favourite was Anemone.

It was amazing how she got away with mischievous things in his presence; he always stood up for her or made her parents change their minds about something she was barred from doing, and she loved him for that.

Mrs Verité had been visiting at the castle on several occasions and really felt like one of the family members. She had some peace of mind, that Jason and Keanan were doing well at the hospital, and they were not allowed out, so she drove over to see them when she had permission. She had called to tell them that she had won the lottery and could now afford to pay a private institution for her boys, but that meant that they needed to go out of Maldavia. It was a serious decision to make and she needed some advice, because leaving the country would mean that she would see less of them.

Eric and Angelique was happy for her, and they advised her to send the boys to the Shomilia's Rehabilitation Centre in Canada, that was equivalent to the Betty Ford Clinic, and they would be healed in no time.

Everything worked out for the best. Anemone was supportive when her mother felt lonely, with the triplets away at their pre-school where they spent every morning. They actually enjoyed being around other children, and they each had complete different personalities.

Murielle had been released on parole, and the charges of abduction of minors were taken off her record because of the lack of proof. She had served exactly three years in prison on a suspended sentence of six years. When she left the prison she contacted no one, and moved from her flat to an unknown place, and no one heard from her for a long time. She had been reconciled with her sister, Indra, who had married Pedro and was living a very unhappy life. Pedro was messing around. He came home whenever it suited him, and he made no secret that he was seeing other women, by the lipstick on his shirt collar or the strange perfume. Indra was hoping that when she told her husband that she was expecting a baby, he would finally come to his senses and grow up to a certain extent, he might even be thrilled.

The Fourbourg family had been going through a difficult phase, while Indra considered herself lucky to be living in a mansion, driving one of the most expensive Ferrari sports cars, and wearing expensive clothes. Her mum survived with the anonymous help she was getting and Indra helped out wherever she could. Now that Murielle was out of jail, she was relieved.

Pedro did not mind Indra helping out her family financially, because money was no obstacle for him, but he hated the scandal that followed the Fourbourg family and continued for eternity. He had made it clear to Indra that he had a reputation to hold up, and his family depended on him. He told her that it was no good for his self-esteem either, because he felt trapped. Pedro was a gorgeous-looking, rich playboy, and Indra was head over heels in love with him.

Pedro had just got home, probably from one of his one-night stands, only to find that his wife had gone out of her way to prepare a dinner by candlelight. Everything was superbly laid out, she had even taken out the silverware and best china for the occasion. It was their first wedding anniversary, and she didn't have a clue of how to tell him that she was pregnant. They had brought up the subject about having a baby on several occasions, but Pedro refused to take part in such a big responsibility, and wouldn't hear about it. Pedro had warned Indra that he didn't like children, and didn't feel like sharing his wife with a noisy brat around the house, and there was no way she would get him to change his mind.

Pedro had walked up to Indra and given her a peck on her cheek before walking straight into the shower. He later appeared dressed to kill. She had been waiting for him in the lounge, where she had prepared a cocktail and some chilled Dom Perignon champagne.

'What's the occasion?' he asked.

She reminded him that it was their first wedding anniversary, and that she was hoping that he would be the one to remember. She offered him a snack of caviar and goose liver paté. Indra got him to do the honours by opening the bottle of champagne. She handed it to Pedro, who felt embarrassed. He didn't really care for birthdays and anniversaries, but he apologised, feeling a bit uncomfortable because he had made plans for the evening, and needed an excuse to leave. He had an hour or two to play around with, so he would stall for time.

They sat down to dine, and she told him that she had an announcement to make, and came right out with it.

'Pedro, we are going to have a baby,' she said.

Pedro looked at her, very surprised at her tasteless jokes. He finally found an excuse to leave the dinner table and bang the door. He acted agitated and told her that he was in no mood for silly jokes, and reminded her how he felt about children.

'You've got to get that silly obsessive idea out of your mind,' he said softly, 'or you're going to regret the day we met and you'll have to find someone else to father your child.'

Indra informed him that there was no sense in getting into an argument because of it, and told him that it was no longer a project, but reality, so it would be preferable if he could take his responsibilities like an adult.

Pedro sat across from her, completely shocked at the news, when suddenly he burst out laughing. 'No longer a project?' he said. 'Whose project? A reality, obviously yours, but I have news for you, you are going to get rid of it as fast as you have made it, and I don't want any part of it, is that understood?'

He laughed, as if she had just cracked the most hilarious joke on earth, then, suddenly, Pedro pulled everything from the table and told her that she was the most selfish person he had ever met, and that having a baby was a decision that needed both parties' consent, and that he had no recollection of ever agreeing to her capricious tantrums. He accused her of being disrespectful towards his feelings and ideas, and that she had broken a pact between them, so he could never trust her in the future. Before leaving he told her to make arrangements to have an abortion as soon as possible, and if she didn't, there was no point in staying married to him, because he wouldn't be able to have intercourse without worrying about the outcome, and then he walked out furiously, banging the door behind him.

Indra was heartbroken, and admitted being selfish about getting pregnant without his permission, but honestly didn't know what to do. If she didn't have the abortion, she would lose her husband, and if she did, she couldn't live with the idea either, so she was in a delicate situation and needed to think carefully. She knew that Pedro's threat about getting divorced from her was genuine. Either way their relationship was doomed. She felt that he was looking for a reason to get out of the marriage anyway.

Indra had stayed home, trying to find a solution to her problem, but she was completely blank. If she kept the baby she would end up a single mother without resources; because she had married him under a pre-nuptial agreement she wouldn't get much out of the whole affair, and what hurt most was that she loved him. After a week of absence, Pedro kindly came home and simply asked her if she had done what was expected of her. When he realised that she hadn't made a move, he told her to pack a bag and follow him.

Pedro took her to a mutual friend and obstetrician and had him perform an abortion on her. Pedro excused himself from the company and told her that he would be in the lobby when she was done. The doctor assured Indra that she wouldn't feel any pain and that as soon as she came to she could leave. She was still under the influence of the anaesthetic when she recovered and staggered out into the hallway, where she expected to meet her husband, but it appeared that he had more important things to attend to than wait for her.

Indra boarded a taxi back home and walked straight into another surprise. At first she thought that she was seeing things because of the anaesthetic, but soon she realised that it was no illusion. The dining room had been emptied of its antiques, vases, dinner services and cutlery, and all their Rembrandt paintings had been taken from the wall. She walked into the other rooms and found that everything else was in place, including her valuable jewellery, but there were no real valuables left in the entire household, so she immediately called the police who arrived and took a statement from her. Inspector Prador assured her that the house had not been broken into, as there were no signs of infraction and they could only think of one thing, that was very common in such situations, and that was that her husband had abandoned her. They would get in contact with him and ask him to clarify the situation, so they could finally sort out their differences.

When they finally got hold of Pedro, he admitted that he had left in a hurry and taken all the family jewels along with him, because he wanted to spare her the humiliation of the abortion and the divorce until later, because he wanted out of the marriage and didn't know how to tell her. He told her that he would come back and discuss things with her when she felt better, but Indra wasn't going to leave things at that; she needed to know what was going to happen to her when he was gone.

He told her that it was senseless to have a court battle, as he had married her under a pre-nuptial contract and that she had too much to lose, so he suggested that they get a divorce, based on incompatibility. She would get to keep the mansion with all its contents, as well as her car and he offered her a lump sum of money, amounting to eight million dollars, and maintenance of one hundred thousand a year for the duration of ten years, or until she decided to get married, when the maintenance would automatically cease. Indra was more than pleased with their arrangement, even though she would have preferred to work out their differences, but he wasn't just leaving her penniless and heartbroken. She knew that he cared for her, and just wasn't ready to assume such a responsibility as marriage, but he was leaving her comfortably off.

Before Anemone's eighteenth birthday party, Alex suffered a stroke and was hospitalised for a long time. Edwina was very worried about his health and stayed at his bedside day in and day out, until he finally recovered. Angelique had insisted that they come and live at the castle until Alex had totally recovered and was ready for action again. They didn't want to be a burden to the children, so they accepted only after Angelique had promised that they missed them and it would be nice to have them for a while.

Antoine had been keeping an eye on their home in Calicorne while they were at the castle, because he was now based there permanently and it was ideal for him to have put aside his travelling to spend more time with the family. Antoine was pretty scarce for a while, and seemed happier than ever; there was something different about him, even his appearance was outstanding.

Antoine surprised everyone one weekend when he was invited to a barbecue at the castle. He brought Indra along with him, and everybody was glad to see her because they hadn't been in touch for a long time. They had a drink together and strolled behind the men playing golf. While the meat was being marinated and the fresh salads prepared, they simply enjoyed the scenery. This was Indra's second visit to the castle and she found it breathtaking, she really loved it.

A little bit later they had all sat down for lunch, when Antoine told them that he had an important announcement to make. Everybody listened attentively, while Antoine told them to welcome the brand new Mrs Indra Lemoin. Antoine informed the family that he had married Indra Fourbourg, in the strictest confidence, and that only her mother was present at the wedding.

Mrs Lemoin was very fond of Indra and would have approved of their marriage if Antoine had discussed it with her, but he chose to do it secretly, so she felt hurt that her son didn't even have the decency to tell her that he was engaged to Indra. She would have arranged to give them a wedding at the castle, in the same way they did for Eric, and even if they didn't want a big do, they could have at least invited the immediate family to the secret wedding. She told him that she was totally disgusted with his behaviour, and that even though the family had their differences, it didn't mean that they would reject Indra; on the contrary, they would have liked her to choose her wedding gifts like any other bride.

Mr and Mrs Lemoin had been in Marula for over three weeks and both Antoine and Indra drove up every weekend and stayed for a day before leaving. Anemone was busy scraping together ideas about her birthday party which was within a month. Indra turned out to be very helpful and Antoine had millions of suggestions which they sometimes found outrageous and laughed about.

They had had a lovely evening playing construction games and ended up playing gin and rummy, when the telephone rang. Everyone was surprised as it was about two thirty in the morning, and who would want to call at such an ungodly hour? Pedro was on the line wanting to speak to Indra, and he sounded out of breath. Antoine didn't like Pedro, and found him very rude. He would have preferred his wife to cut all ties with him, but they had remained friends and he didn't want to play the jealous monster.

Antoine had asked him why he was calling at such an ungodly hour, obviously because he had no respect. But Pedro reminded him that he didn't like him either, but had important information concerning his mum and dad. He got right down to it and told Antoine that his parents' home had been destroyed by a bomb blast and there was nothing left but cinders. While he happened to be on his way home from a party, he saw Paolo's car parked on the side of the road with many other onlookers, and they asked him to call and tell them about the incident.

'I thought you would be grateful, but you do take everything for granted, don't you,' he said and replaced the receiver.

They flew down to Calicorne straight away, and were questioned by the police, who needed all the information they could get. Alex was in a state; he had just had three imported cars delivered from Japan, and had especially made the trip to choose them personally. An open coupé Lexus and a Hyundai, and a Camry as well, on approval. He couldn't believe that it had also been blown up with the rest of the house, but he thanked his lucky stars that his private collection had been taken to the warehouse for preparation for the forthcoming rally in Calicorne. The Calicorne rally was one of the grandest events that took place annually, and everyone attended, especially the cream of the crop, and most of the owners spent more time with their cars than they did with their families.

All the people at the scene were questioned, including Murielle and Paolo, but nobody seemed to know what had happened. There were no casualties, but the damage was extensive. Everything had gone up in smoke. The experts were on the scene within minutes of the blast and got busy immediately, scraping through the debris for some clues to find out what had caused the blast. Eric was certain that Murielle wouldn't get involved in anything to do with the Lemoin family while she was out on parole, but it didn't stop her from hiring someone else to do the dirty jobs, although this time she was being more careful so as not to be caught. But Antoine had a better idea: he asked why they didn't have Murielle followed by a private detective, so they could finally catch her in the act. Eric hated himself for not having thought of the idea a long time before.

The insurance company had been to inspect the debris, and meanwhile, Edwina and Alex moved into one of their apartment buildings. Because the rally was to take place within a couple of weeks, Alex needed to be in Calicorne. He never missed a single rally; three of his cars were purchased when he was only eighteen years old. In his collection he had a fifty-year-old Bugatti, and he looked after it as if it were gold. He had the cars handled by experts only and they were heavily guarded twenty four hours a day.

The evening before the rally, Alex had asked his boys to come along with him to do a round at the warehouse to see his jewels, as he called them. The cars had been tested for road worthiness and were absolutely immaculate. They checked every single car before leaving, and all seven vehicles seemed in perfect condition. He had signed the register at exactly midnight and had left feeling very proud. He could have a good night's sleep and be back at six in the morning to meet the drivers. Alex always met his drivers a few hours before they took off for the competition, during which he stayed in the pit stop area. The warehouse was locked in their presence and everybody left at the same time, leaving only the two security guards and their vicious dogs to watch over the building for the six-hour shift.

At six o'clock in the morning, Alex, Eric and Antoine went along to see the line-up. When they approached they noticed a group of people looking on, and this wasn't normally allowed; something must have happened, so they rushed to the scene and had the shock of their lives. When Alex finally reached the warehouse he looked on at the remains of what was once his prized collection. He wept like an infant. Someone had stripped all his cars right down to the wheels, leaving only part of the bodies; they had removed the doors, the bonnets and even the steering wheels and the car seats. By now Alex was furious. He couldn't understand how someone could have got past the security officers without causing the alarm to go off.

It appeared that the building on the opposite side of the road to the warehouse had gone up in flames, and the security guards heard screaming from that area, so they rushed to the scene and tried to get to the people in the blaze, but the fire was too wild for them to get in, and they called the fire brigade. After the fire fighters had put out the fire, they were told that there were no people in the building, but they had found a tape recording and a loud speaker, meaning that it was planned to attract their attention. The security officers explained that they couldn't have been away for more than thirty minutes after the fire broke out.

Alex was so angry. He tried to say something to the security guards, but never got to finish his sentence, when he fell down to the ground and died of a heart attack. Antoine didn't waste any time. He suddenly punched one of the security guards in the belly and told him that if he had stayed at his post, as was required of him, his father would still have been alive. He chased the guy and told him to get out of his sight and never return. Bobby moved away so fast that he accidentally bumped into Eric, who punched him in the guts as well and let him go.

By now some people had gone to the stands to inform Mrs Lemoin and the others that Alex wasn't well and that he had passed out at the warehouse. Edwina told Mathilde to take care of the children while Anemone, Angelique and herself rushed to the scene, where they found Alex already dead. This was the last thing they expected, and it was very sad indeed, when they heard why he had heart failure.

The ambulance arrived and removed his body on a stretcher, while Eric and Antoine tried to fathom out what exactly had happened. Eric was questioning all the drivers to see if he could come up with some clues, when he saw Paolo. Eric didn't know Paolo very well, but he knew that he was Murielle's boyfriend. He was dressed up in a driver's suit with the Lemoin slogan and monogram, meaning that he was going to drive one of Alex's cars. Eric immediately demanded how he got the job. He explained that he had received a proposition in the post asking him if he would like to drive in the Calicorne rally and that if he was interested he was hired. But they had not specified for whom he would be driving.

Paolo was the best Formula One racing driver in Manshaven, and had won the world championships three times. He always took part in rallies and competitions, and this time he didn't refuse because he hadn't done a Grand Prix for a few months, and speed was his game.

When the police arrived a few minutes later, Eric had already found out some interesting things. Fingerprints were taken from the cars, and samples were taken from all the drivers and security officers.

The private detective arrived at that very moment and handed the photos to Eric. Eric was completely taken aback when he saw the photos. Paolo and Murielle had been on the scene at about three o'clock in the morning when the fire broke out. They had gone along by the side entrance, but there were no security guards or dogs anywhere nearby at the time. They left about twenty minutes later, just before the security guards got back, and got onto a motorbike and left in a hurry. The detective had followed them, but had lost them in a traffic jam.

As a matter of fact, the private eye had written out a full report since six in the evening until six in the morning. Paolo had attended a bikers' meeting down town at six o'clock and had left at seven thirty, wearing blue jeans and a red sweater, with a black leather jacket and biker boots. He returned to his home directly thereafter. An hour later, he came back out wearing black leather pants, a short-sleeved white T-shirt and white and black snakeskin leather boots. He held his black leather jacket over his shoulder. He was accompanied by Murielle, who wore white cheeky shorts, knee-high boots and a boob tube, also carrying her jacket over her shoulder – it was a short white leather jacket.

He had followed them to Ontario's fish restaurant and finally to Tuckers Palace discotheque. They parked the motorbike in the second row from the main entrance door and entered. At about two thirty they came back out from another entrance and got onto the motorbike, wearing their jackets now. They drove towards the warehouse, where they parked for about ten minutes, when suddenly the building next door went up in flames. They drove right in and went straight to the warehouse and parked the bike.

They took at least twenty minutes and then rushed back to the discotheque, and parked the bike in exactly the same parking space as when they first arrived and went back in the same way they came out. It was about four when they left to go home. The private eye had all the photographs to prove it.

Paolo couldn't believe that this was happening, and he looked totally shocked. He told them that it was true right up to the disco, but that they had not left the disco until four in the morning, and they had witnesses that could vouch for them. Investigations were made and the barman, and about a hundred people had seen them all night long. So who were the people who framed them, and why?

The people who came out of the side door certainly looked like them and even had the keys to the bike. They had found no other fingerprints except Paolo's, Murielle's and another female's on his motorbike because the man wore gloves. The photos were not clear enough to prove that it had to be them; they were not seen going into the warehouse, and they had not taken anything from the premises, so the charges against them were withdrawn.

After Alex was buried, Edwina was terribly lonely and missed him very much. She didn't have her home in Calicorne anymore, and now she was a widow and didn't know how she would cope. Angelique refused to let her suffer in silence and invited her to come and live with them at the castle. It did the world of good, because it was so peaceful in comparison to the city, and she loved being there. Edwina had finally found peace of mind, and her husband was buried at the castle, so she went to his graveside everyday.

Shortly thereafter, Anemone celebrated her eighteenth birthday, and only her grandparents were absent, and she regretted not having them there. Anemone was very excited about introducing Marc to Antoine, but Antoine didn't seem too impressed with the boy. Marc du Preez was a very conceited young man, and often gave the impression that he was snobbish and reserved, but once he got to know people he really proved to be different. Antoine thought of him as shrewd, and he advised Anemone to explore before she became committed to any one individual. Anemone just laughed at his remark and told him that he was a little bit jealous, and it was normal, because she was growing up too fast, but he would get used to the idea.

Since Edwina had moved to Marula, Antoine spent every weekend at the castle, and everyone got along very well, as in the past. It made a difference that Alex was no longer present, but Indra had joined the family and played an important role in bringing some laughter to a difficult time, and it was highly appreciated. No one could replace Grandma Lemoin, or Alex for that matter, but life needed to go on, and the pain was eased by the happy moments spent within a very strong and united family.

Anemone was very excited about her graduation party, and Giovanni had come over to see if she needed some help. Even though everything was planned already, she really appreciated his assistance, and liked him very much. They had been good friends for two years now, and he often came to help her with her studies. He had helped her prepare the invitations for her first big bash after her graduation, and they were both looking forward to it.

Anemone depended on Antoine and Indra for a lot of young ideas, and she insisted that they be present at her party. Angelique and Eric saw no harm in it, although they didn't mind if she didn't have any adults at her party, because she was an understanding, reliable and mature girl who took good care of herself. She had good and respectable friends; they liked Marc du Preez, and also took a liking to Giovanni Mancheta, probably because they knew him better than they knew Marc.

Arrangements were being made for the rest of the family to go off to a pleasure resort for three days and leave the freedom of the castle to Anemone, who had turned out to be one of the most beautiful girls in Marula. She was having a lot of success with the boys, but she was a serious girl. Indra had worked with the caterers and arranged the decorations while Antoine chose the wine list and the cheese, and he certainly had a surprise up his sleeve. When the big day arrived, the stands were installed, while trestles and chairs were put up in the banqueting hall. The guest room was closed off, and not even Anemone was allowed in. Indra got dressed and then helped Anemone to dress up, while Antoine welcomed the first arrivals.

When Anemone appeared, she looked gorgeous, and everybody turned their heads to look at her. She wore a red skin-tight silk mini dress, with a low-cut neck line, and she had tied her long blonde hair into a sophisticated chignon with a black headband She looked absolutely stunning. Indra looked just as pretty as Anemone; she wore a blue mini skirt with a turquoise satin top.

The first guests arrived, and among them was the famous Giovanni Mancheta, an absolutely gorgeous creature, who looked as if he had stepped right out of a playboy cut-out. He had the most superb blue eyes, dark hair, cheek dimples and the sexiest body you could imagine. Antoine could not help but compliment on his looks. Giovanni was madly in love with Anemone, but she only had eyes for Marc du Preez, a very good-looking guy, blond, blue-eyed and rather ordinary in comparison to Giovanni, but there was no doubt that she fancied Marc. Both Marc and Giovanni arrived on their own, while the majority of their friends were in couples. Anemone had made the introductions and the party got started. Antoine and Indra had arranged for the seating and had name cards around the dinner table. People were being shown to their respective seats.

When everyone else had been seated, Anemone got to sit opposite Giovanni, while Marc was placed next to Indra, opposite Antoine. The menu consisted of seafood and they had dry white wine. Everybody seemed to be enjoying themselves: they had eaten and exchanged conversation and had finally concluded at the dinner table. They later had the reception and ate some snacks and danced to the disco music. The bar was being opened, and as the majority of people there were moderate drinkers there were no restrictions.

Everyone seemed to be enjoying themselves – even Giovanni had a double whisky and soda – but Marc stuck to his orange juice and excluded himself from the company. Anemone knew that something was the matter, so she asked him what was wrong. Marc told her that he didn't like Antoine, and had the feeling that it was mutual. For some reason he had found a way to separate them at the dinner table, and he was fussing over Giovanni instead. Anemone told him that he was mistaken, because Antoine wouldn't do it purposely to hurt his feelings, but Giovanni was an easy person to converse with, and a lot of fun, and he and Antoine had a lot in common. They almost had an argument about comparisons when Antoine, who had sensed the vibe, came and had a discussion with Marc.

Anemone appreciated it very much, and returned to Giovanni and brought him right over. Somehow Antoine had persuaded Marc to have a drink, and Marc seemed to be having more fun later – he was even laughing at Giovanni's jokes.

The party was booming and everybody was on the floor dancing, when suddenly the music stopped, and Antoine asked everyone to be quiet. He turned down the lights, with the result that everybody stopped in their tracks. The stage curtain had been lifted and the psychedelic lights went on and a band came running onto the stage and started singing a song for Anemone. She couldn't believe it. Antoine had hired her favourite group, Simply Red, and all the youngsters were excited. The majority of the people had been looking forward to attending one of their concerts when they eventually decided to come to Marula. It was a knockout, and Anemone couldn't thank Antoine enough, but he told her to thank Giovanni, because he had called him to suggest that he call the guys to do the show. She hugged him and thanked him very much, and then invited Marc for a dance, and later danced with Giovanni as well.

Some of the people were rather tipsy, including Marc and Giovanni, who got up on the stage and gave the crowd a show, while others cracked jokes at the bar. By the early hours of the morning, some of the people had already left, while others were to spend the weekend at the castle. Giovanni was invited to stay over, and he knew the castle off by heart because he had been a guest on several occasions. He always got to have the blue room all to himself. He loved it because it was sea-facing and he could hear the waves hitting the shore from a distance. Marc occupied the green room at the far end of the first floor corridor.

Antoine and Indra had excused themselves from the company and retired to bed. The others could hardly keep their eyes open. Anemone thanked everyone for the lovely evening and walked up the staircase with Giovanni and Marc, followed by Jessica and Andrew, and they all went into their respective rooms.

Anemone had slept like a log, and she was usually a light sleeper, so she wondered if one drink could have had such a effect on her. She felt odd, as if she had wet the bed. Now this was something; it was not as if she had got skunk drunk. She had drunk quite a bit before, and never slept as deeply as she had that night. She had a splitting headache, but then she realised that she was stark naked and uncomfortable. She never slept naked, and knew that she could not have removed all her clothes on her own. Then she turned over to find her underwear. When she noticed blood all over her white linen sheet she was in a real state of shock, and knew that someone had taken her virginity. She felt ashamed. How could Marc have taken advantage of her, after they had come to an agreement to wait until she was ready? She was totally horrified. Anemone could not believe her eyes. At first she wanted to scream for help and tell everyone that she had been sexually abused, but she knew that it would cause a scandal and Antoine would call the police, and the whole neighbourhood would know what had happened.

Anemone cried and thought that it was very unfair. She had always imagined that having your first sexual relationship would be different and something out of this world, but now everything was ruined. She felt like locking herself into the bedroom and staying there for an eternity, but Indra came and knocked at her door to tell her that breakfast was ready. She replied with a broken voice that she would be right down. She rolled up the sheet and shoved it into the closet, then made up the bed again and then went downstairs.

Her eyes were totally bloodshot and she acted very strangely. Indra worried and asked her if she should call the doctor. When Anemone heard the word 'doctor' she immediately blamed it on the alcohol; she told them that she had gone into a deep sleep and had woken up with a splitting headache, but that everything was okay now. Giovanni and Indra had also slept deeply and had headaches when they woke up. Marc hadn't stayed for breakfast and had been taken home by Luther. Now Anemone had no doubt whatsoever that it was Marc who had taken advantage of her. He had left, afraid to face her, but she would deal with him later.

Anemone spent the day wondering why she hadn't woken up when she was being sexually abused, and worst of all, was that she didn't even know who had done it. Giovanni would never have done something so awful, and none of the other guys could have come into the house, as they were lodged on the east side of the castle with their partners; when she thought that, the only person she could think of was Marc.

Over the next few weeks Anemone refused to take Marc's calls and refused to see him, but he insisted and came over to the castle. She told him that everything was over between them after what he had done. She told him that she loved him and thought that he would be respectful and keep his word, but he had proven to her that he was no good and she didn't want him anymore. Marc was furious at her accusations and denied ever having done something like that, he told her that. He had given her his word that they would wait, so he had no reason to use forceful methods to obtain her favours, because he was not a sex maniac. Marc told her that she had probably been raped by Giovanni, and now *he* was taking the rap. Anemone was shocked that he could even suggest something so awful and told him that Giovanni was her best friend and would never do something so horrible to her, because he respected her. Marc told her that it was clear that she had much more in common with Giovanni than with him, and that she was better off with Giovanni. Anemone accused him of being jealous and envious, and told him he was being a louse for not being able to own up that he had drugged her and then taken advantage of her.

She told him to leave, but after some thought, he told her that he too had woken up in the morning not remembering a single thing from the time they went up the staircase to their rooms. He told her that he apologised for what had happened to her, if indeed he were responsible, and that he would prove his respect and marry her, because he loved her. He said it was true that he was jealous of Giovanni, because he spent more time with her than he should as a friend – there was no doubt that he was in love with her too. Anemone cried and told him that she needed some time to think about it, and it would be better if they didn't see each other for a while.

Anemone had been brooding for a couple of weeks, and Giovanni had noticed that she had become mature and different, and he told her that she could tell him everything, and he promised not to tell. She told him exactly what had happened and of Marc's accusations concerning him. Giovanni had tears in his eyes. He told her that he loved her so much, and was still hoping that she had broken up with Marc so that he could be the first, but he didn't even know that they were not having a sexual relationship, and it sounded rather unlike Marc to do something like that out of spite, he just couldn't understand. Giovanni told her that he was going to break Marc's neck, and he didn't want her to see him again. She told him that she had broken up with him already, but she never wanted him to even mention that they had had this conversation. Angelique had also noticed something different about Anemone and asked her about it, but she told her mum that she was preoccupied about which university she was going to. She didn't feel like going overseas. Three days later Angelique and Mrs Salmino were going through the linen closet to remove the old sheets and towels and replace them with new ones she had just bought, when she came across a sheet that had been ruffled into a ball. That was unusual, as all used sheets went into the laundry bin. How come this one ended up in the closet?

When they finally folded it to put it with the laundry, they realised that it was blood-stained and Angelique immediately knew what had happened, and went down to see Anemone for an explanation. Anemone burst into tears and told her mum that they had drunk too much and were not aware of their actions at the time, and now they both regretted it. Angelique took her daughter to the doctor, and she happened to be pregnant. This was a total disaster; they were looking forward to her going to university to study medicine, but now it was out of the question. She was expecting a baby at the age of nineteen – what a disappointment.

Angelique informed Eric, and the only decent thing left to do was to inform Marc and his family. Marc was prepared to shoulder his responsibilities and marry Anemone right away, but that would mean giving up his studies, and he had just received a letter telling him that he had been accepted at the University of Stamford and it was a chance of a lifetime – all the best professors and doctors were at that university. Eric and Angelique had encouraged him to do his doctorate and then think of marriage later. Marc felt that it would only be proper to give his child a name before he left to go to Stamford because he would only get to see them twice a year. Anemone told him that there was no rush and that they would talk about it within a year or two.

Anemone had become officially engaged to Marc, leaving Giovanni heartbroken, but Giovanni had no intentions whatsoever of breaking up his friendship with Anemone, and he still had hope that he could convince her that she was making the wrong choice, because he was willing to marry her even though she was pregnant. In the meantime Marc got ready to go to Stamford University, and would do his utmost to come home at least once or twice a year for the next seven years. Giovanni rejoiced when he heard the good news; finally he was going to spend every spare minute with Anemone, and in the process he would conquer her heart in Marc's absence, and maybe she would realise that she didn't love Marc after all.

Giovanni had become accustomed to taking Anemone for long walks in the forest and on the beach. She was very lively and always did outrageous things such as riding bicycles, but Giovanni watched her carefully, and saw to it that she didn't get injured. He especially liked going on their Sunday picnics, as if it were going to be that way for ever.

When Romeo was born, Marc had special permission to fly home and witness the birth of his son. It was a great event, and the little boy was the spitting image of his mum, with the same gorgeous blond hair and blue eyes. Anemone and Marc had thought that Antoine would be very pleased if they asked him to be Romeo's godfather, but they didn't want to offend Giovanni, and explained to him why they felt that it would be correct. Giovanni agreed wholeheartedly, and joked that he would be the father of the next one. Anemone just laughed. Antoine was totally thrilled to be Romeo's godfather and simply adored the child.

Romeo was very fond of Antoine, but had a preference for Giovanni, and Antoine became irritated, and reacted in an overly possessive manner towards the child. Giovanni understood why Antoine reacted the way he did, simply because he couldn't have children of his own. Antoine treated Romeo like his very own son, and sometimes went overboard; he took full advantage of the fact that Marc wasn't available. Giovanni had tried to keep a low profile, to give Antoine the impression that he was very important to Romeo. Antoine really appreciated it, and their friendship had improved tremendously.

Antoine drove up to Marula every weekend to spend some time with Romeo, while Giovanni had the whole week to take him to the zoo or a circus or teach him to ride a bicycle. Giovanni had even bought him a puppy that got strangled some time later. Romeo adored Giovanni and called him Gio. It often happened that Antoine had to call off his weekend visit because Anemone and Giovanni would go on a picnic or a fishing trip, and he would insinuate that they were having an affair. Giovanni told him that he would have liked to, but Anemone was engaged to Marc and he had no chance. He wasn't going to give up that easily however.

When Romeo celebrated his fourth birthday, Marc had come home, having taken three months off to go on a long holiday with his little family. Marc felt that he needed to get to know his son and he intended to have him to himself for the whole duration of three months. Anemone thought that it was a great idea, and she didn't mind getting away herself, so they left both Antoine and Giovanni to lick their wounds. They kept in touch and sent postcards and photos to the whole family, but Anemone kind of missed Giovanni and phoned him every other day. Marc didn't like it at all, but she assured him that Giovanni was her best friend and it was going to stay that way.

While they were away, numerous incidents had occurred at the castle, and Angelique and Eric got back to worrying about the safety of their children; it was very unpleasant. Leonardo and Angelo had been playing close to the little water dams on the golf course, when suddenly a man came out from nowhere and pushed the two of them into the water and ran off. Angelo hated water, and couldn't swim at all, while Leonardo managed, but he wasn't an ace either. Leonardo had surprised everyone with his life-saving skills he used to save his brother's life. No one knew that he could swim, and that he had been doing a secret life-saving course. While he was learning to swim he had asked the physical training teacher to keep it a secret, until he got his certificate of merit, because he wanted to surprise his parents. Angelo was panic-stricken, but his brother dragged him out of the water and performed mouth-to-mouth resuscitation, saving his brother's life. The gardener, seeing that Leonardo was on his knees and Angelo seemed to have been hurt, ran over to see what he could do, but apparently Leonardo had already taken care of his brother, and he was very shaky. They couldn't identify the man because they had their backs towards him.

Since then Angelique didn't let them out of her sight and always made sure that they were surrounded by adults. One Sunday afternoon, Leonardo was at the pond trying to fish with his father's fishing rod, while Giovanni, Eric and Antoine played a game of cards. They had been closely watched by the adults, who seemed absorbed in their game of cards, when a few minutes later they realised that Leonardo was nowhere in sight. They called for a search, and found the boy hanging from a tree, with his mouth taped up so that he couldn't scream. They got him down just in time, before he suffocated.

They had called in additional security guards, to accompany the children to school and back. For a few weeks everything went well, until Leonardo went missing again, but this time for three whole days, and they couldn't understand how he could have disappeared so fast. They had searched the whole castle, and there was no trace of the boy. Angelique was mad with worry; she knew that someone was out to kill her boys, so she prayed that he was safe somewhere close by.

Indra had just pulled up, and seeing that there was a problem, took part in the search. When they had searched the entire area there was nothing more they could do than sit and wait for the police to find the child – or his body. Anemone had phoned and was told what was happening, and she decided to cut short her holiday and come back immediately.

Antoine had been preoccupied himself, and it was evident that he was having domestic problems of his own. Indra tried to pretend that all was well, but any fool could see that they engaged in an argument. Eric wasn't any better. Someone had attempted to kill his sons and now Leonardo was missing for the third day. He didn't know what to do. Eric had served himself a double shot of cognac, and passed the bottle to Giovanni, who accidentally dropped it on the floor. He apologised for being so clumsy, while Eric told him that Luther needed to go and get a few bottles of wine, so he could bring back some more cognac. Luther had scarcely got to the cellar when he was back asking everyone to follow him. Eric asked him what had happened, but he just kept on saying, 'I found him, thank God I found him.' They ran to the cellar, knowing that he could only be talking about Leonardo. Angelique was so happy when she saw that her son was well, and that he had survived for three days locked up in a type of grotto, because he couldn't even get to the cellar.

Leonardo told them that he had followed Luther to the wine cellar and crawled through a pipe to get to the grotto, from where he watched Luther do the wine list. Leonardo knew that he would be at least twenty minutes, so he didn't rush to get down. All of a sudden he was pulled down and knocked over the head. When he woke up again, everything was completely black and dark around him, Luther was no longer there and he must have been out for at least thirty minutes. Someone had put a handkerchief on his nose, that is why he passed out.

'I promise that there was someone else in the cellar at that time. I'm sorry, Mum, but I have been doing that for a long time, and nothing ever happened before. I would go up into the cave and eat some of Grandma's blueberries and canned fruit secretly and then disappear through the hole adjoining the main door before Luther left, only this time he had just popped his head into the cave, and the door fell shut, or so I thought. I know that it was daylight when I felt the knock on my head and I woke up when it was completely dark and black in there. It took about an hour to find the light, and I screamed with all my might, but no one seemed to have heard me.'

He told them that when it became dark he left the light on and he had a feast by eating the smoked ham and blueberries. He drank apple cider and mineral water; he even had the idea to defrost the smoked sausages and open up spare bottles of mustard and ketchup. He could only complain about one thing though, that he had to cover himself in the thick greasy blanket, with potato sacks as pillows. He slept quite well, as there was an old carpet he managed to turn into a mattress.

Eric was so relieved. He asked Angelo whether he was afraid that no one would find him. He proudly announced that he didn't worry too much; there was enough to eat and drink, and he knew that Antoine or Luther would come into the cave some time or another, as they did at the end of every month, and it was the twenty-fifth, so the longest he would stay was six days, and he had enough food and water for a long time, but the person who knocked him out didn't know that – he intended him to die of cold, hunger and fright.

Angelique was sincerely proud that a child of his age could fend for himself in such circumstances. They were happy to have him back home safely. Angelique and Eric discussed the matter and came to the conclusion that something fishy was going on and that everything that had happened recently was by no means a coincidence. They lived in fear and were heavily protected; they had even installed a laser security system, and had hidden cameras all over the castle.

Eric thought it would be a great idea if Antoine and Indra stayed at the castle on a permanent basis, and they both agreed. Antoine could go to Calicorne twice a week to check up on his business, and he was sure that Indra would be happy. Indra was thrilled and couldn't wait to move into the castle.

Anemone had got back, and Marc had returned to varsity. The family was reunited; Edwina was happy to have her whole family together, and all was well. The next few weeks Indra wasn't feeling well, and she consulted Doctor Portnoir, who told her that she was pregnant. She couldn't believe it, knowing that Antoine was sterile, but the doctor explained that it was rare that something of this sort happened, but it was possible. They did some check-ups on Antoine and found that he had regained the ability to father children. He was terribly excited and later found out that it was a little girl, and he cried with joy, even though he so dearly wanted a little boy of his own. He told everyone that they would have another baby soon afterwards.

Anne was born while Anemone and Marc's wedding arrangements were underway. Marc had attained his doctorate in medicine and needed to practise at a hospital for another year before he could go into private practice. Anemone had always dreamed of having a white wedding and she wanted Giovanni to be her usher, while Marc decided on his best friend and colleague, Xavier, to be his best man.

The wedding was to take place at the castle within a couple of weeks, and Anemone and Marc needed to discuss where they were going to live after the wedding. Marc told Anemone that he was no parasite and didn't want to live with his in-laws, that it would create problems in the long run and they wouldn't have any privacy. He also thought that it was time to give Romeo a little sister or brother, so he was expecting her to accept the home that his parents had offered them as a wedding gift. Anemone told the family about her decision to go and live in the house that Marc's family had offered them, and everybody was disappointed; they had been hoping that the castle would stay in the family, but when they realised that there was nothing they could do to convince Marc, they just left it at that.

Giovanni, on the other hand, knew that Marc was a selfish bastard and didn't really care about what Anemone wanted, and he wished he could make her understand, before it was too late. He also knew that it meant, seeing Anemone and Romeo on certain occasions only, and they had become part of his life. He knew exactly what they needed and how to take care of them, but she was marrying Marc. Giovanni had tried everything in the book to talk her out of the wedding, but she told him that she was obliged to marry him because he was her child's father, and that she liked him very much. Giovanni asked her how she could be marrying a man she only liked, while he would do anything to make her happy; she knew that he loved her, and he was convinced that she loved him too. He was afraid that she was making a big mistake.

The kitchen tea was being held at the castle while Marc had his bachelor's party in his apartment. He had invited Eric, Giovanni, Antoine, Luther, André and Mrs Verité's two sons, who had become friends with them recently, and all the freshmen and doctors he had been with at university. Anemone had Indra, Angelique, Edwina, Mrs Verité, and some of her friends and the ladies from the women's club. After Anemone had opened up her presents, she decided to call Giovanni at Marc's place and ask him to meet her at Jingles discotheque later in the evening; she felt that it was only fair to spend the evening with her best friend, knowing that she wasn't going to see him as often as she would have liked to once she moved into the house.

It appeared that the boys were having a lot of fun when she called. Marc was occupied with a call-girl that the boys had ordered for his last night as a single man. Giovanni later told Antoine that Anemone had called him and that they were to meet some place, so he had to leave. He told Antoine that he would see them at the wedding, and that Marc wouldn't even remark that he had left. Giovanni was wrong about Marc not noticing his absence. When he enquired where Giovanni had gone, Antoine told him that Giovanni had something urgent to see to and that he had left a message, wishing Marc a pleasant evening, and said that he would see him at the church.

Anemone and Giovanni had a great time. They returned home at about four in the morning, but regardless of what time it was when they arrived, they still had a nightcap together and chatted for another hour before going to bed. Anemone woke up at about ten o'clock and had some breakfast with Giovanni and her parents before Giovanni went away to get dressed.

When Giovanni excused himself from the table, Eric could see how difficult it was for both Anemone and Giovanni to leave. Eric made a remark that even stunned Angelique. He said, 'Now that's a man with all the qualities a woman could wish for. I wish I was having him for a son-in-law as well.'

Anemone just shook her head and told her father that she couldn't marry two men, and that she loved both of them in different ways, and that she had made her choice.

The guys had just got back from their night out, and it was clear that they had had a great time. They had already had breakfast and a shower, and they needed to return to get Marc to come along with them to Marula; they wanted him to see his wedding present before the ceremony, otherwise it would have to wait for the next day, and they preferred to get it over and done with. They were to pick up Giovanni on their way.

When they arrived at the apartment Marc was already up and ready for action. They told him that they needed to show something to him and then they would bring him right back. When they had driven for a while, they blindfolded Marc and told him not to peep. They finally reached their destination and joined the others who were waiting for them. Marc descended from the car, still blindfolded, when Eric asked Giovanni to do the honours. Giovanni read the little note, as follows:

To Marc, this is our way of welcoming you into our family, and the token herewith means that it won't be all play but hard work and fun. We have the honour of offering you a surprise and wish you a long and happy marriage.

Giovanni helped him remove the blindfold and Marc almost fainted when he saw the building.

Giovanni carried on and said, 'We have the honour of handing to you, your very own D & L du Preez Medical Centre,' and then handed him a pair of scissors for him to cut the ribbon that surrounded the building. Marc didn't know what to say; he was completely taken aback by their generous gift. He thanked them sincerely and asked Giovanni to join him; he hugged and shook hands with Giovanni and handed him one side of the scissors and they cut the ribbon together. It was tradition to break open the top of the champagne bottle against the wall, and he did just that. Xavier had brought a big bottle of champagne, and they drank directly from the bottle, and hummed all the way to the car and back home. Marc hadn't seen Anemone, and wasn't allowed to until she walked down the aisle.

Marc realised that he had to get ready for his wedding within five hours, but Antoine, Eric, Mr du Preez, Xavier and Giovanni just carried on singing all the way back to his apartment. They were not totally sober, and still recovering from the hangover of the previous evening. Marc was in a rather naughty mood so he offered them some whiskey, but Giovanni told him to be reasonable, and that he needed to relax for a while and then get ready, and that they would see him at the church in a few hours.

When they had left, he realised that he had forgotten to pick up his tuxedo from Top Hat, in Marula, so he rushed towards the car, asking Xavier to take any calls. Just then he noticed two teenage boys tampering with his car, no doubt wanting to steal it. He put his hand in his pocket to remove the keys and realised how absent-minded he had been – he had left the keys in the ignition. He screamed for them to go away but they simply ignored him and carried on. There was no way he could reach them in time to stop them, because he was quite a distance from where they were. They jumped into the car and started the engine. Within seconds they were blown to pieces. A bomb had been planted in the car, and if he had reached the car he would have been killed. There was no doubt that it was meant for him. He walked back into the house all shaky and trembling. The police had arrived and so had Antoine, Giovanni and Eric, as well as Mr du Preez – they had been alerted by Xavier.

Marc was in a terrible state, and Eric asked him if he wanted to call off the wedding, but he wouldn't hear of it; he wanted to get married today, and no killer was going to spoil the best day in his life. Marc was trembling like a leaf, and he asked Giovanni to pour some whisky while Antoine got some ice from the kitchen. Xavier had gone to the toilet while Antoine got the ice. They all had about two drinks, and ensured that everything was okay before leaving. They felt assured when the Cadillac pulled up and was waiting out front to drive Xavier and Marc to the church. Giovanni felt uncomfortable leaving Marc in Valdover, and enquired if he didn't want to come and get dressed at his place – maybe he would feel safer.

Everyone had left when Xavier told Marc to shake a leg and get done as they were to leave within an hour. So Marc got into the bath, while Xavier lay out his clothes on the bed. Time was running out and Marc was in a hurry. He had got into the bath when he realised that he had no soap or even a face cloth or towel, and he thought he had put some there the previous night. He called out to Xavier, who denied putting away anything at all. Xavier got a towel from the closet and handed it to Marc, but he needed soap and shaving mousse as well. Xavier didn't waste any time; he reached for the soap on the holder and threw the soap at Marc who had his back towards him, and then reached for the shaving cream. Suddenly the holder came down. He heard a click and noticed an automatic switch on the panel, but before he could stop the dryer from falling, he slipped and fell partly into the bath. The hairdryer fell into the bath and electrocuted both of them.

In the meantime, back at the castle, Anemone was getting ready to be accompanied to the church, and everybody else was ready. The wedding was to take place within thirty minutes and Mr du Preez made a call to the apartment to see if Marc and Xavier were ready, or if they had left. He was quite relieved that the phone rang continuously, and took that to mean that they were on their way. Half an hour had gone by, and the congregation was becoming impatient for the groom to arrive. Mr du Preez assured them that they must have been caught up in some traffic or something and that they would turn up in the next few minutes – which turned out to be hours. When they hadn't arrived an hour later, they phoned and still had no reply. Mr du Preez was furious. If Marc was being irresponsible he was going to teach him a hard lesson, so he got into his car and drove away from the church. Angelique and Mrs du Preez told the guests that they were welcome to come over to the castle and have something to eat, that the church ceremony was called off, and that there must have been a good reason for Marc not turning up. All the people who knew Marc agreed, so they drove up to the castle and continued to have a party while waiting for some news.

Anemone wept with embarrassment, while Giovanni tried to pacify her. She could not believe that he would do such a thing to her. She just did not know what to think.

Eric and Antoine had followed Mr du Preez to find out what had happened. When they arrived at the apartment, they noticed the Cadillac parked in the driveway, but the chauffeur had disappeared, and Xavier's car was in the driveway too, so they knew that Marc had not left the apartment to go to the church, or any place else. They went up the staircase, and knocked at the door. When no one answered, Mr du Preez pushed the door ajar and entered. He called out to Marc who did not seem to be home. Antoine and Eric sat down, while Mr du Preez went through the apartment to see if they were asleep, when suddenly they heard him screaming. They both jumped up and went to see what he had found. They went into the bathroom, and saw the two bodies.

The police arrived, as well as some relatives. Eric called the castle to let them know what had happened. An investigation was opened and the bodies were taken to the mortuary. The entire case was bizarre. Inspector Klaus put it down to accidental death, but Eric wouldn't hear of it. He told them that earlier that day Marc's car had blown up, killing two teenage boys, and that it was too much of a coincidence for two fatal accidents to take place on the same day. The bomb was certainly meant for Marc himself. Mr du Preez thought something was peculiar. He knew Marc was very cautious and would never have taken a hairdryer or any other electrical appliance into his bathroom. It was for that reason he always used a razor blade. Secondly, he never used a hairdryer and, as far as he was concerned, Marc never even owned one.

The detectives found a plug with an automatic starter, meaning that with the slightest movement the dryer would have gone on automatically. It was really too ridiculous to assume that he would dry his hair while he was in the bath tub. They had also noticed that there were no towels or face cloths in reach apart from the one that Xavier held – even the toothbrushes were placed in the cabinet where the dryer came from. There was no doubt that someone had purposely put away Marc's toiletries so that he was obliged to get them himself. He could have saved his life if he had not got into the bath before realising that all his things had been put away. But they hadn't put aside the possibility that someone might have come into the flat while they were in the bath or in Marula.

Inspector Klaus had opened up a murder investigation, and questioned all the gentlemen who attended the bachelor's party. The neighbours were questioned as well, and the staff at the castle. They looked at everyone who might have had a motive to get rid of Marc, and came up with Giovanni as suspect number one, although everyone else was suspected too. The main suspects were those who saw Marc hours before his death and on the morning of his death: Eric, Antoine, Xavier, and Giovanni. They had all kinds of theories about what could have happened.

Inspector Klaus suspected that Marc might have been living a gay life and was involved with Xavier, who had a hard time accepting that he was going to marry Anemone. Back at the university people remarked that they were very close and had shared the same apartment. Xavier was insanely jealous, and it ended in a crime of passion.

Everyone listened attentively, and no one was allowed to comment until the inspector was through. As for Giovanni, who had always been in love with Anemone, since she was only sixteen years old, he tried to persuade her to break up with Marc and marry him instead, and made no secret about trying to talk her out of the marriage. When Giovanni realised that within hours Marc was to marry the only girl he had ever loved, he schemed to kill him and pacify Anemone until her wounds were healed, and then he would ask her to marry him.

Eric had no motive whatsoever to kill his future son-in-law and rather liked him, to judge from the wedding present they had offered him the day he died, unless it had been planned to confuse the investigations. Antoine did not get along with Marc, and they had several arguments concerning Romeo. He could have wanted to kill Marc because he was going to take away his nephew, as they were to move into the house offered to them by Marc's family.

Months had gone by, and Giovanni was having a hard time trying to prove his innocence, but because he had left the castle earlier in the afternoon, before the bachelor's party, he could not have removed the hairdryer, because Antoine, Luther, André and Eric picked him up on their way to the apartment. Anemone had used the hairdryer minutes before they left the castle, and remembered not finding it later. So anyone could have taken it as there were many people coming to and fro – there was a combi full of Marc's friends who had met at the castle, from where they drove off together.

It was extremely difficult to find the culprit, as they were dealing with some fifty people. There were good friends, and there were others who envied Marc, while others still only pretended to like him. The murder was thoroughly planned, and they had not left a clue to help unwind the puzzle along the way, with the result that they were back to square one, and Marc's family wanted things to be left that way. It was in memory of their unique son, who they believed had an unlucky accident.

Giovanni's name was cleared of all allegations and he was acquitted, but Giovanni was convinced that Marc was murdered. He told the inspector not to close the case for a while, that they might find the murderer when he least expected it. Anemone believed in Giovanni's innocence from the word go; she knew that he had absolutely nothing to do with Marc's death. Anemone went through a painful period of grief, while Giovanni helped her along by being a father to her son as best he could, and it was pretty easy because Romeo worshipped the ground he walked on.

After a few months, the novelty seemed to have worn off. Giovanni thought that the time was appropriate to propose to Anemone, so he invited her to a romantic dinner by candlelight and popped the question, and she accepted without a second thought. Giovanni said a prayer for Marc, and thanked the Lord that she had accepted his proposal. Giovanni couldn't wait to tell everyone the good news, when he accompanied Anemone to the castle.

The first thing he did thereafter was to contact his dad in Italy, to let him know that he was getting married. He wanted his father to arrive before the big day. He spoke about Anemone and Romeo, but Franco felt as if he had known them for years, because she was the only conversation they ever had, and he was very happy that they were finally going to tie the knot.

A few weeks later, Giovanni's father was a guest at the castle, two weeks before the big day. Franco Mancheta was a real gentleman, and everybody took a liking to him. He was just as good looking as his son. Angelique was curious to know whether Giovanni's mum was attending and when she would arrive. Franco told them that he had tried to contact her, but that they had lost contact over four years ago, but he was doing his utmost to find her.

The wedding was absolutely marvellous and Anemone looked stunning. She never thought that she would be this happy, but it felt as if she had wasted so much time, and that she should have married Giovanni a long time ago. She hadn't realised that she actually loved Giovanni, and that she would have done the wrong thing by marrying Marc, so finally everything turned out for the best.

After the wedding, Franco stayed on for another week and then had to leave to finalise some business he had left unattended. He promised to be back as soon as possible, and told them to hurry and give him another grandchild – he had already adopted Romeo as one of his own. Enrique was born a year later, and looked just like his father, even though he had his mother's blonde hair, and Romeo was glad to have a little brother. They had a fantastic relationship. Giovanni loved his wife and children, and they were a model couple, meant to be together.

Giovanni had noticed that Antoine always interfered and created arguments concerning Romeo's education and upbringing. Giovanni put a stop to it by telling Antoine that he was acting in a very childish manner and that it wasn't going to solve any of their existing problems. It was not like they needed to compete for who was giving the most attention and love to Romeo, and what the child needed most was stability. If the rivalry between themselves continued the child would end up confused and then they would have a real problem to deal with. Giovanni told Antoine that nothing had changed; he could carry on taking Romeo on fishing trips and he could see him whenever he felt like doing so, but they needed to compromise, so that there would be no offence when the child chose what he liked to do most. Giovanni concluded that it would be in the best interests of Romeo if they were more like friends and not enemies.

Shortly thereafter the miracle happened. They were having a barbecue when Indra made the announcement that she was pregnant again, and this time they were going to have a baby boy. This was really something to celebrate. Edwina didn't know what to say, other than to congratulate them, while Giovanni thanked his lucky stars that finally Antoine would have his own son to pay attention to, and Romeo would become a normal child, with adoration for his baby brother. Edwina said a little prayer and knew how proud Alex would have been if he were present. Grandma Lemoin would probably have told him, that nothing was impossible with prayer.

Indra gave birth to Antonio and Antoine was the happiest man on earth. He adored his son and called him Tony, like his granddad had always called him. Antoine went from one extreme to another: he constantly told Indra to be careful with Antonio's little head, and wanted everyone to treat Antonio like a porcelain vase. He loved Anne, but really overdid it with his son, and his feelings for Romeo stayed the same. He acted slightly differently, by being kind to the other kids, but clearly he had a preference for Romeo.

Giovanni knew that he had participated practically in the upbringing of Romeo, and that he was the godfather after all; that was why he felt that he had a say in everything that concerned Romeo, but he didn't realise that Romeo was confused and asked a lot of questions. Giovanni had made a point of speaking to Anemone about the matter, and told her that they needed to move out of the castle if they wanted their children to have a natural and stable upbringing. He also told her that he was referring uniquely to Antoine. Anemone told him not to be hasty. She knew that Antoine meant well, but she would point out to him that he had children of his own and would get him to lay off. She told Giovanni that it would be heartbreaking for her parents if they left now, and if there was anyone who should be leaving it was Antoine.

After they discussed the matter, things went from bad to worse; even Angelique and Eric had noticed that Antoine had changed and deliberately upset the apple-cart. He spent more time trying to tell others how to live their lives than occupying himself with Indra and their two children. They had endless arguments that needed to be solved with family discussions, so Anemone told Antoine that if things didn't improve she was going to move out of the castle. Antoine could take a hint and told them that if there was anyone who didn't belong there it was him and his family, and she didn't have to worry, they were going to move. He apologised for the inconvenience he and his family had caused, and concluded sarcastically that the castle wasn't his anyway. Eric wanted to say something because of his remark, but he realised that Antoine wanted him to feel guilty but he wasn't going to fall for it this time.

Antoine pretended to be hurt and blamed it on Giovanni. Within a month Antoine had moved out of the castle, and back into their home. It was probably the best thing that ever happened to him. He often invited Enrique and Romeo to come along when they went fishing or camping and he was very proud of Antonio. Indra adored seeing Antoine play his fatherly role, and she knew that it was probably the only thing he ever really wanted out of life – to have a boy of his own – and she had really noticed the difference since Antonio's birth.

Some time later, Antoine found out that Anemone was having problems with Mr and Mrs du Preez. She had received an official letter from the minister of justice, informing her that Mr and Mrs du Preez had filed for custody of their grandson, and they all needed to appear in court within a few days. He was furious that they hadn't informed him about something so important; after all he was Romeo's godfather. Anemone told him that he was not obliged to know everything about Romeo, because Romeo had parents of his own.

When they appeared in the supreme court Mr and Mrs du Preez told them that they refused to settle it out of court, because they had been refused visits and holidays with their grandson. They had no alternative, but to file for visiting rights but that was refused too, so they filed for custody. Anemone was furious because she had never deprived them of seeing Romeo whenever they wanted to. As for holidays, they were always through Romeo's own choice.

Angelique made a point of telling them that it was ridiculous that they wanted to take the child from his parents and his cousins. She told them that she thought that they were better people. She really wasn't expecting such behaviour from them, and there was no way that she was going to allow them to get away with it. Mr du Preez explained to her that Marc was their only son, and that Romeo had told them that he wasn't going to see them as much as he had before, because he had his own family who he wanted to stay with, but he refused to tell them who had imprinted such things on his mind. Romeo had told them that it was his own idea, and that he was sorry if he hurt them. The du Preez family didn't change their minds about adopting their grandson, and called upon a lawyer to represent them in the magistrates' court.

Some months later, while the case was pending, having failed to hear from the du Preez family, and their final appearance at the magistrates' court, there was a warrant for contempt of court and some officers went to their home and found them hanged in the lounge. The story made the headlines and for months Anemone had to deal with journalists following her and Romeo.

It was really tragic. It was clear that their home had been broken into, and that there was a struggle. They had been taken into the lounge, where wooden beams hung from the ceiling. Their assailants had brought together two chairs, and forced them to stand on them side by side. A rope had been flung around the beam, and noosed round their throats; the chairs were pulled from under their feet, strangling them both to death. The assailants had generously helped themselves to their private belongings – the safe had been broken into as well.

One day Romeo had come from school with an injury, but his mum fixed it with some antiseptic and a band aid strip. However, it seemed to worsen. It was really causing concern, because every time he just bumped himself he turned blue and it would turn septic, and he often became feverish. Giovanni was very worried and took Romeo to the doctor. At first they could not find out what he was suffering from, so they carried out further tests and finally concluded that he had contracted a little-known disease called meuclesia, which is a rare blood disorder which can eventually lead to leukaemia. He needed a bone marrow and tissue transplant. They were advised to make a worldwide call for donors because his father was deceased and his mother wasn't compatible.

Romeo needed a lumbar puncture very urgently, and needed intravenous drips to prepare him for surgery – if they should find a compatible donor. They knew that his father had passed away, and that his mother didn't have the same blood group, so they took samples from other family members, and found that Antoine was compatible. At least they could prepare him for the transplant while waiting for a donor – if they could find one that is. They had called on parents and children around the world who could be donors, but there were thousands of children dying everyday because they could not find a suitable donor.

Anemone had her hands full, and had a long battle to fight, scared that her son was getting weaker by the day and that if he didn't get a transplant as soon as possible he would die. Giovanni had tried to help, but he was incompatible too, and they needed to keep their son alive.

In the meantime, the doctors had informed her that they might have found a donor who wished to remain anonymous, and if he were compatible they would contact them later in the evening. At seven the phone rang, and the doctor had given them the good news that they had found a donor, but he wished to remain anonymous, and they should sign a document agreeing that they accepted that. The doctor asked them to come in straight away and have Romeo admitted. They were obliged to respect the professional part of not being furnished with the donor's particulars and regretted not being able to thank him personally.

The operation was a success and Romeo recovered as if he had just had influenza or something mild. He was discharged, and Melany had been seeing to him while they waited for Angelique and Anemone to get to the hospital. Anemone couldn't wait to get him home, but Angelique hadn't seen Melany for quite a while and told her to go along, while she stayed to enjoy a cup of coffee with Melany. Melany had called Angelique on several occasions, and hinted that she had something important to tell her, but she just never got round to it. Angelique remembered that she needed to speak to her about something. Melany pretended that it had slipped her mind, and that it probably wasn't important at all. They parted and promised to see each other soon.

The following week, Barry and Melany came up to the castle for lunch and had a lovely afternoon. Just as they were leaving, Antoine, Indra and the kids pulled up, and they greeted one another and then Barry and Melany left. Antoine told Angelique that the lady's face looked familiar, but he didn't know who she was. Angelique just laughed and told him that she was her best friend since she had opened up the ladies' club.

One day, Angelique was sort of craving for fresh cream pastries and she knew of no one else who could do them as deliciously as Melany, so she called her and ordered a dozen. Melany brought them round and ended up staying for supper. She had been trying to get Angelique on her own, but they were interrupted every time she tried to catch her attention. Melany decided that she wanted to have a chat with Angelique at their favourite coffee shop, Les Flavours, where they made a date and met the following day.

Angelique arrived at the coffee shop, and found Melany stuffing herself with fresh cream pastries. She didn't give a hoot about her chubby figure because she had this thing about sweets, and Angelique found it very funny, and laughed about it. They sat down and had an interesting conversation about what had occurred during the previous months, when Angelique remembered that she had been on duty the evening that Romeo had his transplant and mentioned how fortunate they were to have found a donor for Romeo, and that it was a pity that the person wanted to remain anonymous. Angelique knew that she would succeed to convince Mel to tell her who the donor was.

'Melany, I know that this is asking too much, but it's very important for us to know the identity of the person who donated his bone marrow to Romeo, and seeing that you were on duty that evening, you surely know who the person was.'

Melany was glad that Angelique had actually brought up the subject, because she had been trying to find a way to tell

Angelique. She reminded her that such information was to be withheld from anyone else and if she was telling her it was because she wanted to from the first day and had finally plucked up the courage to do so. Angelique pleaded with her, saying that she wouldn't contact the person involved, but at least if she knew who it was she would feel a lot better. Melany told her that she was better off not knowing, because if she knew it would change her life and she would be shocked. Angelique told her not to be silly. How could anyone so generous shock her by doing a good deed? Melany then told her that the specific evening they were preparing the donor, she was surprised to see who it was, and really thought how generous he was, until she overheard the conversation between the treating doctor and the donor.

Earlier that day they had done tests on the donor to see if he was compatible or not and the results from the lab turned out to be much more than they were expecting. It had actually become rather confusing because they had compared Marc's file to that of the donor and found that Marc du Preez couldn't have been Romeo's father, because the donor had more than one similarity genetically, whereas Marc had none. They had done other genetic tests thereafter to double-check and found no doubt that the donor was Romeo's biological father. So why had Anemone and Marc lied about something so important?

Melany told Angelique that she was asked to leave the room at the patient's request. She later went into the recovery room, and, noticing the door was slightly ajar, she eavesdropped. She had already seen the results, but they didn't know that. The doctor told him that he was aware of what was going on, and that such information needed to be placed on the child's file; in case of accident or death it was essential to know both parents. There was nothing Antoine could do but ask the doctor to be discreet.

Melany knew that she would lose her licence to practise, and that if things leaked out she would be history in the medical world, but since she had gone so far, she might as well get it over and done with. Angelique didn't have a clue who it could be, because Giovanni had been with Anemone all the time they were doing the transplant, so it couldn't be him. Angelique was tired of playing guessing games and told Melany to tell her who he was. Melany told her that Antoine Lemoin was the biological father of Romeo, and they were lucky that he wasn't born deformed at all because of the incest.

Angelique couldn't believe it. She was terribly upset, and knew that something needed to be done. This was incest, how was it possible that Antoine had sexual intercourse with his very own niece and blamed it on an innocent boy, and why didn't Anemone ever say something about it. The two of them could not have been in their right minds. Why did Anemone believe that Marc was Romeo's father? Suddenly it occurred to her that her daughter would never have allowed it, and he must have raped her. Surely there needed to be an explanation and she was going to find out.

Angelique knew that she had a tough job to handle. First she needed to get hold of the medical file, and then she had to talk to Anemone and find out what exactly happened. Angelique had been in all sorts of predicaments before, but this one needed to be handled very delicately, because she was sure that Anemone didn't know the truth. There was only one way to find out, and that was by telling Giovanni about it. It might cause problems in their relationship later on, but she had to take the chance.

When Angelique finally got home she was in such a state that she wandered around for hours, doing everything but achieving nothing, thinking of how she was going to break the news to Anemone. Instead, she found herself asking Giovanni to meet her in town at Les Flavours. When

Angelique arrived, Giovanni was already waiting, and knew that it must be important, otherwise she would not have asked him to come to town. Angelique asked Giovanni if he knew anything about Romeo, and if Anemone confided in him. Giovanni replied that Anemone was distraught after what happened and told him what she suspected. It appeared that Marc had drugged her, and taken advantage of her while she was asleep, without her consent.

'I offered to break his skull, but she stopped me and told me that she had already broken up with him, and that bit was true because she didn't see him for over two months, until she discovered that she was pregnant and they got back together again.

'In the beginning Marc denied having done this to Anemone and accused me of raping her – that is why she broke up with him. He later apologised and accepted his responsibilities. You know, even though I didn't approve of Marc for Anemone, I got the feeling that he wasn't the type of guy who would take advantage of a girl, especially when he had promised to wait until she felt ready for such a relationship. It is amazing what drugs can do.'

'You're damn right about that,' she said. 'Marc didn't touch Anemone, he was right about her being raped, but not by you; it was her very own uncle, Antoine. The son of a bitch took away my baby's virginity and got her pregnant, leaving her to believe that an innocent boy was guilty. Meaning that she might not have married him anyway and then he would still be alive and well somewhere out there.'

Giovanni couldn't believe it and admitted having had thoughts in that direction when Antoine started meddling in Romeo's well being, but he had thought of himself as far-fetched and silly. Giovanni told Angelique that he was going to teach Antoine a lesson he would remember for the rest of his life, but they were not to react hastily, not until they had spoken to Anemone, because she needed to know the truth and the sooner they did it, the better it would be.

Angelique tried to be very diplomatic about it, so she started with the day she found the sheets in the closet. 'Anemone, do you remember the night Romeo was conceived?'

'Of course,' she said angrily, as if she had trodden on unfavourable memories, and, exactly as they were expecting, Anemone found it distasteful of her to bring up such a delicate subject when Marc was dead. It wasn't the fondest memory she had of her graduation party. She also told them that she had already fallen in love with Giovanni at that time, and when she realised that she was pregnant by Marc, she had already closed her heart to him, but she knew that there was no turning back.

Then Angelique asked her how she could have been so sure that it was Marc who sexually abused her under the influence of drugs and that it was unlike him. Anemone then remembered Marc denying having done any such thing after they had discussed it between themselves, but later he apologised and told her that he wasn't sure of anything either, and that he probably was the one who did it while he was under the influence of drugs.

Anemone didn't like the conversation and wanted to know why they were asking so many questions and why Giovanni had told her mother that she had been sexually abused. Angelique told her that Marc had been sincere when he denied not having had sex with her, and that she would have to be strong, because what they had to tell her was monstrous, and it was going to hurt her very much, but it was important that she be told.

Anemone immediately understood what they were insinuating, and had a rumbling tummy. She demanded to know, if Marc wasn't Romeo's father, then who the hell could have been so cruel to do such a bad thing to her?

Angelique didn't want to prolong the agony, so she came straight out with it and told her that Antoine had drugged both her and Marc, and then taken advantage of her when she passed out. Marc was confused because he knew that he didn't do anything, but because he too was drugged, he could not give an account of his actions.

When Romeo had his transplant, Antoine was his donor. The blood tests showed that he was Romeo's biological father. Anemone was totally hysterical, and she had passed out. They needed to calm her down by giving her a sedative. Giovanni promised his wife that he would personally ensure that Antoine paid for what he had done to her, but Angelique told him to keep out of it. Angelique told them that she knew exactly how to hurt his pride. After they had spoken for a while, they decided not to inform Eric, because there would be war, and Eric would kill him instantly and his mother wouldn't survive the blow, and might suffer from a heart attack and die. Angelique told Giovanni that she was taking the law into her own hands, and that he could be an accomplice if he wanted to, but she didn't want him to get involved personally.

Angelique, Anemone, Giovanni and Romeo got into the car while the other children were being minded by the caretaker and Edwina. They drove over to Indra and Antoine's home. It was clear that they were not expecting anyone, because Indra was keeping the children busy around the swimming pool, wearing a G-string swimsuit, and Antoine would never have allowed her to wear it in company. Anemone and Romeo joined her, while Angelique and Giovanni excused themselves to see Antoine who was busy building a boat for his son, in the backyard.

Antoine was surprised to see them, because they never came by without calling first, and this looked urgent, because tears were flowing down Angelique's face. Antoine rushed over and enquired about what had happened, and pulled out a bench against the tree and asked her to sit down. Giovanni told him that he was the one who needed to be seated, because he was the one who was going to need the whole bench when they were through with him. Antoine laughed, thinking that Giovanni was cracking one of his tasteless jokes as usual, but he obeyed without hesitation and sat down. Then Angelique moved toward him, and started by asking him if he remembered a rape that took place in the castle on Anemone's graduation day. Antoine looked shocked and was quite taken aback.

'Of course, yes, I remember that Marc had sexually assaulted Anemone that night, but only when she announced her pregnancy.'

'You lying bastard, you couldn't have known that. Anemone told no one except me, because I found the blood-stained sheets.'

Antoine became worried when Giovanni slapped his face, and told him to tell the truth before he put a bullet into his head. Antoine insisted that he had nothing to do with it, but Angelique had a better idea. She got Giovanni to remove Antoine's clothes, and tie his hands to the back of the bench. At the time Giovanni did not know what Angelique had in mind, but he knew that it was going to hurt because she was furious. Angelique kept on repeating that Antoine had raped her daughter, and that she was convinced that he tried to rape her too, several times. He was going to pay.

She removed her mobile phone from her bag and made a call to the hospital. She called an ambulance, and told them to hurry as she gave the address.

Giovanni had no idea what Angelique had in mind, but, before he could stop her, she had already slit Antoine's genitals, and left him screaming in agony. She reminded him that it was incest that he had committed, and that she did not care whether she went to jail or not, but now he had what he deserved. She also concluded that the rest of the family didn't know about the incident yet, but it could go public if he messed up and that it was in his best interest to keep it quiet.

They walked away, towards the gate, meeting the ambulance and the doctor, who asked where the patient was. Giovanni pointed to the back yard and got into his car and drove off. The doctor asked Indra what was wrong with her husband, but she couldn't tell because the last time she saw Antoine he was alive and well. Then she heard him screaming for help, and, he was bleeding profusely so she insisted on alerting the police straight away. He stopped her just in time.

Indra needed to get the children back into the house, because they had already seen too much. Their father was naked and it appeared that someone had amputated his family jewels, and it was awesome. Antoine was rushed to the hospital and an emergency operation was being done while Indra waited in the hallway. They operated on her husband, and she wanted to call and find out why Giovanni had done something so cruel to Antoine, but, before he went into surgery, he had asked her not to contact anyone until he had told her what had happened. A while later, Antoine regained consciousness, and Indra was at his bedside and she demanded an explanation. She told him that Giovanni should go to jail for doing what he did, and even if Antoine did something to offend him, why was Angelique his accomplice and why didn't he want to call the police? Antoine told her that Giovanni had not done anything but undress him while Angelique took away his pride, and she was going to regret the day she decided to do it, because she was going to pay very dearly. Antoine told Indra that it was a long story, but he couldn't tell her why.

The tissue and membrane were totally damaged, and they couldn't repair his genitals, so they were partially amputated, and he would never be able to have a normal sex life. The doctors had informed Indra about his state, and she was heartbroken for Antoine and thanked the Lord that they already had two adorable children, but she told him, that she was his wife, and that she had the right to know what was happening. Antoine refused. Indra told him that it proved that he was guilty of doing something awfully disgusting to have provoked Angelique to do what she did. Indra threatened to go to the castle and find out for herself what had happened and then maybe they would finally call the police, because it was the cruellest thing anyone could do to another person, and especially as it was someone he had loved once. Antoine saw that he wasn't going to succeed in keeping it from her.

'I have been accused of raping Anemone, the night of her graduation, and that is untrue. They didn't even give me a hearing for a minute to defend myself,' he said, with tears rolling down his cheeks.

'But that is ridiculous, honey, everybody knows that Marc got her pregnant against her will. But to accuse you of something so grotesque, I think we have to clarify the situation immediately,' she said.

Antoine told her that it would cause a big scandal and that was the last thing he needed right now. Indra looked at him and told him that she was sorry about what happened and Angelique would always have it on her conscience that she had deprived someone from living a normal life and she needed to be punished. Antoine agreed wholeheartedly and told her that they would discuss the matter as soon as he was discharged from hospital, but she wasn't to mention anything about it to anyone, including Eric and his mum; because he didn't want them to worry.

Indra knew that something bad had happened, because Angelique would never have done what she did without valid reason, and wouldn't make allegations concerning her own daughter if they were untrue. There was only one way to find out, and that was to go and speak to her personally.

While Angelique explained the situation to Indra, Antoine was being bothered by the press. Somehow or other the news had leaked out, and the television had also been alerted. It turned out to be one of the biggest scandals. He was being accused of raping a young girl, who had been involved in sawing off his tools and had left him in misery and disappeared. The press went as far as reporting that the girl was under age and her family wanted her to remain anonymous, because she had taken justice into her own hands and he deserved it.

People had manifestations in front of the hospital, with banners reading, 'Well done, you should have taken it completely off'; others saying that chopping it off as capital punishment would keep men at home, and it should be legalised if young girls needed to be protected because men like Antoine were a danger to the public.

Indra had now been enlightened about what Antoine had done and realised that he had lied to her from the word go. He must have been sick in his head to commit such an act. She would never trust him again. She felt sorry for Anemone and they thought about what they would tell Romeo when he was a grown up one day. Luckily he had a family that loved him. It was really heartbreaking to know that Indra had been in the same bed with a man who had sexually abused a member of his family. Indra was married to a monster and it was hard to believe, but the proof was there. Indra cried and didn't want to see Antoine. She didn't bother to see him, but was obliged to when Edwina found out on the news, and rushed to her son's bedside. Edwina knew that there was a misunderstanding. Antoine wasn't capable of hurting a fly; he would never have done it to a minor.

Antoine explained that the girl in question mistook him for someone else. She was crazy because he hadn't left his home that day. Eric told him that he needed to clarify the situation and clear his name, so they called a press conference at the hospital. Indra was terribly ashamed when Antoine lied without batting an eye, and didn't even feel remorse for lying to the whole republic. She hated him, but she had given her word to Angelique that she wouldn't let on.

Antoine's life became a misery from that moment on. An article appeared in the newspaper, informing the readers that the famous Antoine Lemoin had been admitted to the Maltive Clinic, where an emergency operation had been performed on him after he had sexually abused a minor who wished to remain anonymous. The victim, whose name was being withheld for security purposes, had revealed to a family member that Mr Lemoin had raped her, and she had simply cut off his family jewels so he wouldn't get the opportunity to hurt someone else in future.

At first Antoine was relieved that everyone was buying his story, including his mum and brother, and Angelique wouldn't dare say anything, so he could lay low for a while without any problems. Antoine was discharged from hospital, but he needed to be escorted by police protection. People insulted him while others threw things at him, telling him that he deserved to be hanged by his butt. When they reached his home, another surprise awaited. He found infuriated people at the entrance; windows were broken and people were stark raving mad. They didn't want a rapist in their neighbourhood, and he was being threatened. Things got out of hand and they were forced to move from their home.

The children were nervous wrecks and Indra jumped up every time she heard a sound and felt worried about their safety. Edwina felt that the least they could do was to have Antoine and his family over at the castle until things quietened down, but Angelique immediately put that out of the question. There was no way she could put her children through another ordeal of threats and the castle would be visited by strange people out to get Antoine and involve his family. It was unlike Angelique to put someone off in dire need, but there was always a first time for everything, and they knew that it didn't seem right, but they respected her wishes.

Eric found it strange that Angelique had become hostile toward Antoine, since the incident. Even though Eric agreed that he could not stay in the castle, he insisted that Angelique had something against Antoine and she wasn't telling him why. Angelique told him that she didn't want angry mobs coming to disturb the peace at the castle and her words were justified, because shortly after Antoine and Indra left their abode, leaving all their belongings, their home was totally bombed to the ground, and it could have occurred at the castle.

Since the incident, they were forced to move three times, until the novelty eventually wore off. Edwina had not seen her son for four months and missed him. Angelique couldn't bear being under the same roof as Antoine, but sooner or later Antoine was going to visit his mum and she would have to put up with it. Some time later Indra had brought the children to see their grandmother and Antoine arrived about an hour later, surprising everyone except Angelique, Anemone and Giovanni. As soon as he arrived he greeted everyone and acted as if nothing had ever happened, and Angelique almost had a fit with his self-righteous performances in her sight. She despised him and couldn't bear looking at him without feeling a desire to strangle him. Anemone had left as soon as he arrived.

The first thing he always enquired about was Romeo, and Giovanni started getting fed up with his so-called godfatherly concern, so he informed Antoine that Romeo had parents who loved him and that he didn't have to be furnished with every detail about the child, and that Romeo was getting ready for an outing with his family.

Antoine looked at him and said, 'You've got to be joking. How can you take the child out when I have driven hundreds of kilometres to see him?'

Giovanni told him that he had gone too far and that he had better steer clear of Romeo and his decision was final.

Eric was completely taken aback. He couldn't understand how everybody could have changed towards Antoine in such a short time, and he felt that they were treating him badly, and he needed things to be clarified. He told Giovanni that they needed to have a meeting concerning all the mystery going on around there. Giovanni apologised for not being able to stay for a meeting then, because he needed to go someplace and the meeting would have to wait until he got back. When everybody had left, Eric and Antoine had a good conversation and Eric convinced him to talk about why everybody reacted the way they did towards him. Antoine told Eric that he was entirely to blame; he had been paying too much attention to Romeo and they had been having arguments about that, but it wasn't that important and he would be more discreet the next time. Eric was relieved when he finally got the explanation he had been waiting for. Edwina apologised for their behaviour, and told Antoine that they weren't expecting him to call that day and that they had already made plans. Antoine told her not to make excuses for them; it was evident that they didn't want him to see Romeo and he didn't know why. Eric interrupted and told him that he knew exactly why he wasn't allowed to see Romeo. Even his mum knew that he had been overdoing it with Romeo so he didn't have to make excuses for himself.

When Giovanni got back, Antoine and his family were still around, so he came down while Anemone and Romeo went to the bedroom. Angelique joined them and greeted Indra, who sympathised with Angelique, knowing that it must have been difficult for her to pretend that nothing had happened whilst Antoine took advantage of the situation. Indra thought that Angelique was being very courageous; she would never have been able to handle it.

Antoine persisted on bringing presents for Romeo and he called whenever he wanted to. Eric had noticed that Giovanni never stayed in their conversations for too long, and Anemone simply refused point-blank to be under the same roof with Antoine, but Eric still imagined that it had to do with Romeo and their last argument, and hoped that it would blow over soon enough and they would become friends again.

Angelique had no choice but to accept his visits, even if it meant putting on an act towards the person she hated the most. She thought about ways to keep him away from the castle, and warned him to keep a low profile, but he just ignored her wishes and almost daringly suggested that there was only one way she would succeed in keeping him away, and that was by telling everybody what had happened, because he wasn't going to keep a low profile from his grandmother's castle to please her, or anybody else for that matter, because Romeo was his son and he loved him. Angelique had warned him that he was going to burn his fingers. Antoine was no longer scared about anything leaking because he knew that nobody else knew about it. After all they had managed to keep it secret thus far.

One month later, Angelique got an unexpected call from Melany, who hadn't been in touch with her since their last meeting, although they had spoken on two other occasions.

Melany told her that she had baked some fresh cream pastries and had no one to share it with and that the coffee was ready, so she expected her within an hour. Angelique was rather bored of sitting around and doing idle things and so she was glad to get away.

When Angelique arrived at Melany's house, the front door was ajar; she had probably left it open for Angelique to enter, so that's exactly what she did. Angelique smelt the freshly baked biscuits and the aroma of the coffee beans. She noticed that the table was set for two, so she called out to Melany, warning her that she had arrived, but Melany didn't answer at first, so she sat down and helped herself to a fresh cream pastry. Suddenly she heard Melany calling her from upstairs, inviting her to join her in the bedroom.

She walked up the staircase, still holding a chocolate eclair in one hand, and pushed the door saying, 'What are you doing in here?'

Seeing all the clothes sprawled out on the carpet, Angelique entered but Melany was nowhere in sight, and it seemed that someone else had been waiting for her instead. Before she could turn to check the other room, a man abruptly closed the door behind her and told her not to scream, while he held a gun at her head. He ordered her over to the bed and forced her to undress herself immediately if she didn't want to get hurt. Angelique had no alternative but to do what the man expected of her and she panicked but there was nothing she could do – it looked as if the man would not hesitate to the pull the trigger. He was a very big-built man, reeked of perspiration, and he had tattoos all over his body – he even showed her a tattoo on his buttocks, of a dagger and a sword. Angelique knew that she had to do exactly as she was told if she didn't want to have her head blown apart. When Angelique enquired where Melany was, the man simply replied that she had gone to meet the rest of her family in some garden he could only dream of going to. Angelique didn't quite understand what he meant, so she decided not to pursue the conversation.

Suddenly he tied her hands behind her back, and beat her up brutally and then sexually assaulted her, carrying on for over an hour. Angelique had prayed to God that he wouldn't shoot her when she suddenly heard doors being locked from downstairs, so she took it for granted that Melany had returned from wherever she had been, and hoped that she would have the idea of calling the police. But the man took no notice of what was going on downstairs, he just carried on, he scratched her and kept on slapping her until she was in tears. Angelique tried very hard not to think about it, and prayed that he would get it over and done with. Then he slapped her and untied her from the bed, and left her stark naked; he bundled up her clothes and walked out of the room with the revolver in his hand, telling her not to move.

Angelique was trembling when she heard the man and his accomplice unlock the back door and leave. She went over to the wardrobe to get a dress and some underwear of Melany's, when a body came tumbling down towards her, and she realised that they had killed Melany. She screamed so loudly that onlookers on the street came closer. She opened up the window and asked them to call the police.

Within minutes the police were on the scene. They took a statement from her, and called Eric who arrived in no time. She told them that she could identify the man who had done this to her and that if they caught him, he had left with all her clothing. Melany's body had been removed after Barry came home to find Angelique completely disfigured, but alive. Eric had gone along and accompanied Angelique to the district surgeon's office, and then she was admitted to hospital. She needed to undergo an operation for nasal bone reduction before she was recognisable. A sample of the man's spermatozoa was taken from her and studied, and she needed to do several other test for AIDS as well. After having had a smear she was discharged some time later.

It was one of the saddest days she ever had to face when they buried her best friend. Angelique had a feeling that she was the cause of Melany's death. It was evident that it was planned for her to visit Melany that day, because she was forced to call her and then make a tape recording of her own voice coming from the bedroom. The assailants had come to her home with the intention of killing her because Angelique had been furnished with information only she could have known, and Angelique was to be punished by being raped and injured because she had destroyed Antoine.

There was no doubt in Angelique's mind that Antoine was behind all of it; he had killed her friend when he found out that she was the one who had furnished the information, and he was dangerous. She needed to make him regret the day he was born, and she was going to make him suffer. He wouldn't know what had hit him. The first thing Angelique did was to inform Indra about her suspicions and warn her to keep an eye on him, while she found a way to keep him completely out of Romeo's sight.

Murielle had just got back from Brazil where she had married Paolo, and they moved back into the family home they had once owned before all the trouble started. Indra was very happy to see her sister after such a long time and she made a point of spending more time with her. Mr Fourbourg had repented and was happy to move back into his home. He paid three times more than the actual value, but he didn't mind because that was where all his children were born and grew up and it was of sentimental value. Francisca was happy to get back as well although she couldn't say that life had been treating her badly otherwise.

She loyally waited for her husband to come out of jail where he stayed for several years.

Mr Fourbourg had paid his debt towards society and wanted to make a clean break, and was always well informed about certain things. He knew that Alex had passed away, and that his sons were handling the businesses. He had only one thing in mind when he left the prison, and that was to recuperate his fair share and everything that was rightfully his, now and in the past. He felt that the business was still partly his, and even if they had managed to delete his name from the contract, he would find a way of getting it back somehow.

Mr Fourbourg did not mind using his daughter to get hold of what he was after. Because Indra was married to Antoine, Mr Fourbourg managed to get important information regarding every move in the company, and he knew that Antoine was no big brain in the business, and that he employed people with no real inclination for the job; all he ever cared about was to see that he was making a handsome turnover, that the company turned out to be profitable and earned him a little fortune. He didn't really care how his employees took care of it, and he really only checked the books on a yearly basis.

Mr Fourbourg, knowing a bit about Antoine's personal problems, didn't hesitate to find false documentation. He started getting involved with the imported goods. He had become friends with real crooks while he was doing time, and they promised that if ever he needed them to pull off innocent little jobs, he shouldn't hesitate to call on them – and he did just that.

Every time Antoine had goods or cargo arriving at the cargo bureau it was checked and off-loaded at his warehouses without any problems, until suddenly they noticed drug shipments. He got called in and was being blackmailed, and the crooks were demanding large sums of money. Antoine had no choice but to pay, because his blackmailers were doing exactly what Mr Fourbourg had done to his father. He couldn't make a move because the thugs he had got involved with seemed to know much more than he had anticipated. This carried on for about a year and it felt like an eternity to him. He had tried to talk the guys into being reasonable, but he was losing his company and couldn't do anything about it. He had no more cash flow, demands were being made that he pay all the debt for merchandise he thought had been paid for. When he had no other solution he consulted Eric and told him that he had got into some trouble and needed financial help. Eric financed the difficulty, but he couldn't get involved in the company, as he had three others to run, so Antoine had no excuses, but had to assume his own responsibilities.

For a while things seemed to calm down, but a few months later he was right back to square one, and completely bankrupt, and found himself in so much debt that he just wanted to get rid of the company. Indra had noticed that he had problems so she asked him what was happening. Antoine told Indra that he needed to sell the company before Eric heard about it, but he wasn't going to find a buyer to take over all his debt. He could obviously afford to pay the debt but he couldn't carry on the way things were going right now. He mentioned to Indra about finding a buyer for the company and that she wasn't to mention anything about it to Eric, or anyone else for that matter. Indra told him that he should sell the company back to her father, knowing how much he wanted to have it. But Antoine told her that she must be joking, he wouldn't be able to afford it anyway and he wouldn't want his father to turn in his grave about it. Antoine told her that she was crazy, she knew how his family felt about that, but Indra had another argument, that if he advertised the sale, Eric would get to know about it, because his approval was necessary, as well as his signature. If her father bought the company, he could falsify Eric's signature, and no one would know until it was too late. Antoine realised that Indra was right, so he told her that if her father was interested he would sell the company to him. Indra told him that her dad was still bitter about the problems the company had created, and she doubted if he wanted to have anything to do with it, but she would talk him into buying it although she warned him that her dad didn't have a fortune. Antoine told her that he had serious problems, and that if he didn't sell the firm, things were going to be tough. She spoke to her dad, who agreed to borrow some money from Paolo and buy back the company. Indra had also given a substantial amount of money towards it and he could afford it easily. The deal was concluded between Mr Fourbourg and Antoine, with Eric's signature falsified.

Several months had gone by before Eric found out that his company had been sold to the enemy and that his signature had been forged by his brother. It was a slap in the face, and a dishonourable thing to have done in memory of Alex. He needed to do something fast to get back L & F, so Eric called Mr Fourbourg and told him that he was willing to negotiate with him, and that he had an interesting proposition to make. Eric wanted to take ownership of the company, even if it cost him three times more than the original price. Mr Fourbourg told him that the company wasn't for sale; even if he offered a thousand times the price, he wouldn't accept. Business was booming at present and he implied that he intended to make up for lost time.

Eric began a lawsuit, trying to recuperate the last thing his father had left to both of them, but Mr Fourbourg had his priorities straight, and there was no way he could recover the company. He finally gave up and became estranged from Antoine because of him falsifying his signature, and because of that his mum found out about what had happened. Edwina had a heart attack and almost died, so they kept Antoine away from her.

Angelique had gone to Calicorne to visit Mrs Verité, who was still living in her spacious home, and had remarried since their last meeting, while her sons had got married too and moved away from home. They often came to see her, whenever they could. Angelique and Mrs Verité started talking about how destiny played its role and how it had happened to be by pure coincidence, that Mrs Verité's destiny came about. It all happened when Mrs Verité had been invited to Anemone's wedding, but she was unable to attend because she was seeing her sons in another town that day. Under normal circumstances she wouldn't have missed it for the world, but she hadn't seen her boys for a while, and they were just recovering from their drug abuse. When she returned from her trip, Angelique brought down the wedding albums, and intended to invite her over for a few weeks. Before they looked at the wedding photos, Angelique saw a photo of a handsome boy on the dresser, then she noticed another, with the boy and his father – she had no doubt that it was Giovanni and Franco. She immediately asked Mrs Verité if she was related to the people in the picture. Mrs Verité, started by telling her about an affair she had had with an Italian doctor named Franco Mancheta, before Giovanni was born. They met while she was on the run from her violent husband, who ill-treated her, she suffered bruises and needed to see a doctor, so she consulted him. He was sympathetic towards her when she told him that her boyfriend, had brutally assaulted her and that she was running away from him. Franco told her that he lived on his own and had a very big house, and that if she wanted shelter, she would be safe at his home. Mrs Verité did not hesitate for one second and moved into the handsome doctor's house.

The doctor was unmarried and had been in practice for only a few months. He was working at a private clinic on a temporary basis until he could establish a practice of his own. She lived with him, and fell in love; she became pregnant and had a little boy whom she named Giovanni. Giovanni's father was an honest and good man; he was very rich, and wanted to marry her, but she always found an excuse and hated living the lie she did. She had got very close to telling him that she was married, but circumstances didn't permit her. She was already married and Franco might have asked her to leave if he found out that she had lied to him, and she would have nowhere to go to with her baby, and if her husband found her, he would put the baby up for adoption and probably kill her.

Mr Verité eventually tracked her down, and fortunately for her Giovanni was safe at home with his father. Mr Verité forced her to go and get her clothing and told her that they were to board a plane within two hours. She lied to him and convinced him that she couldn't go back there and tell the people that she was leaving. They would beat her up as she owed them months of rent. They were drug addicts and they would probably want to sell her clothes for drugs. She told him that she preferred to leave the rest as she owed them some rent money.

They left Italy and flew back home. When they finally arrived he told her to make herself comfortable while he had a shower. She waited for the shower to go on, making sure that he couldn't overhear her conversation, and she called Franco. He was very glad to hear from her, and was very worried and wanted to contact the police, afraid that something might have happened to her. Mrs Verité explained everything to him. Franco told her that he would help her get a divorce and wanted to come and fetch her straight away, but she wouldn't give him her address, and told him that she would contact him whenever she could.

Later she contacted him at every spare moment, but never called from home in case Mr Verité traced the calls. Franco couldn't do anything about it, and wasn't going to part with his son. He promised to take good care of Giovanni and told her that he loved her and would wait for her for as long as was necessary. Mrs Verité had opened up a private postbox and forwarded her address to Franco, who in return sent photos of Giovanni and himself and she did likewise.

Mrs Verité had tried everything in the book to convince Mr Verité to divorce her, but he simply threatened to kill her and then commit suicide thereafter. No other man was going to have the opportunity to have her.

Some time later she was pregnant and this time nothing could make him want to leave; instead he forced her to get pregnant a second time when Jason was only a few months old. Franco was heartbroken and wanted to find a way for her to divorce that evil man, but he watched her like a hawk. They kept in touch and Mr Verité never found out about their relationship or Giovanni, but he had made her life a misery until he died.

Mrs Verité had lost contact with Franco because he had written to tell her that they were moving to Brazil and that she could come and see them under a pretext of some kind, but he didn't know that Mr Verité had passed away, because she hadn't had news from him for four months while her husband kept her under lock and key. When she finally went to collect the post, the postbox had been demolished, and she hadn't been notified because she hadn't left a forwarding address and Franco was paying for the postbox all the time. She had gone to the local post office but the post had been returned to sender.

She had advertised and searched for years, then she had to move into the house she was living in with her two sons from Mr Verité. Until one day she heard that her son was an actor and that he was married to a wealthy lady. She had overheard a conversation about some family which she realised now had to be Lemoin, because they were saying that Giovanni Mancheta was gorgeous and Annie was lucky to be marrying him. She didn't bother to ask them which Giovanni they were speaking about, because she was sure that she had misheard.

Mrs Verité told Angelique that she would do anything to see her son again. Angelique removed the photos from her bag, and showed them to Mrs Verité, who couldn't believe it. It wasn't possible, her son had married Angelique's daughter. When she found out that it was Anemone, she was so happy that fate had worked such wonders. She immediately packed a bag, and drove along with Angelique.

Angelique didn't inform anyone that she was coming, so they were all surprised when Mrs Verité walked in. It was a day to remember. She walked in and Giovanni immediately got to his feet while Franco ran over to her and embraced her. They knew who she was. There were tears of joy and a lot to talk about. Giovanni removed photos from his wallet that his father had given to him, and he found that his mum hadn't changed one bit; she was more beautiful in person and they were going to make up for lost time. He had photos of her when they were together which he always kept in his wallet. They got to their feet, and both hugged her tightly and told her that she was still as pretty as ever. Everybody was happy and Giovanni was relieved to have finally met his mother in person. He was looking forward to meeting his brothers as well.

It turned out to be a successful family reunion and Anemone was pleased that Mrs Verité, who used to spoil her with home-made caramel and chocolate fudge, turned out to be her mother-in-law. Franco sold his businesses in Brazil and moved in with Mrs Verité and married her.

Antoine had been going from bad to worse and decided to go out on his own one night. He was enjoying himself on a boys' night out, and had already had one too many. He listened to cool music and the atmosphere was quite warm and welcoming. He felt that he had drunk too much beer, and he felt like having something stronger anyway, but first he needed to use the men's room. He lit a cigarette and poured some water over his face to freshen up, when some hefty looking gentleman approached and went about doing his own thing. Antoine wasn't in the mood for company so he went into the loo, and was followed by two of the men who stopped him from locking the door. He was being molested at gunpoint, and one guy held a rifle to his temple, while the other spat all over him. The tallest of them all called out to the fatty to finish him off. Antoine thought that they were going to kill him, but he soon realised that they had other intentions first. They tied him up while their friend performed a sexual act on Antoine, and every time he made a move they slapped his face. There were about six of them and each one took their turn. Antoine felt humiliated that he had just been raped by six different guys. They untied him and left him sitting exactly where they found him.

When he finally realised what had happened, he had already passed an hour in the loo. He reacted rapidly, pulling his clothes back on, and left in a hurry. He went straight home and got into bed after he had had a shower for hours on end. Indra saw him getting into his nightgown, and headed for the bedroom. She went over to him and asked him what was the matter, but he answered her abruptly, by telling her to mind her own business. Indra didn't like being treated that way, so she reminded him that they were invited to a birthday party; she told him that she was going with or without him. Antoine wasn't keen on letting her go on her own, but he had no alternative. After all that had happened to him he was hurting, and was too ashamed to let anyone know about it. So he let her go, while he cried and licked his own wounds. In the state he was, it was preferable to call a doctor but he couldn't bring himself to do so.

Indra had met up with her sister and ran into Pedro, who'd become good friends with Paolo, so they had a long chat, and kept each other company for the evening. Indra and Pedro had renewed their friendship and became close friends. The following morning Antoine saw photos in the newspaper of his wife and her ex-husband and freaked out with jealousy. He couldn't stand seeing Indra with another man, even if he was her ex. They weren't having sex, so he worried that she might give in to Pedro, but he had to be careful as he needed her more than ever, and even if she was having sex with Pedro, there was nothing he could do.

Some weeks later, a man rang the doorbell and Indra answered. The man wanted to know if Antoine was home. She asked him who he was so she could announce him to Antoine. He told her that they were very close friends and that she must be Indra, and that he was pleased to meet her, and that all his close friends called him Hitman, and that Antoine would know who he was. Antoine overheard the gentleman and came out straightaway. He immediately asked Indra to excuse them and invited the man in. Indra went into the kitchen while they were having a conversation. She knew that he was trying to make the man leave but the man felt like staying, so she decided that she was going to come on in and make Antoine introduce her to his friend. Indra sensed that he was uncomfortable; she poured them some drinks and Antoine was drinking more than usual. Then she played a little game to find out who this guy was.

She said, 'So your friends call you Hitman. Boy, that is interesting. How many people did you hit in your lifetime?' she asked, joking, and burst out laughing.

Both Hitman and Indra chuckled with laughter when he replied 'hundreds'. Antoine chipped in and told her that he did not appreciate her stupid jokes and that his name was Jack, but before he could go any further the two of them laughed again, saying, 'Jack? Jack the Ripper.' This time Antoine became annoyed. He asked Jack to leave and told him that he would contact him, and that they would have a game of golf together sometime. Indra told him that she was delighted to have met him, and that they were having a party the following Saturday, and that he was welcome to come along with some of Antoine's other friends as well.

By the time Jack left Antoine was so angry that he actually slapped his wife, and then realised that he had gone too far, so he apologised, but she was not going to allow a man to beat her up, and did not accept his apology. She got into her car and drove off to see Pedro, as the children were spending the weekend at the castle. She came back home the next morning. He made up with his wife and told her that he was sorry and that Jack wasn't an honest man and he could mean danger to the family. She didn't insist on wanting to know all the details when she realised that he wasn't telling her why he was scared of Jack.

Saturday arrived and Jack turned up with seven blokes and sexy young female company. Antoine played along because he had no choice. The party was in full swing, he knew all the men, and when the party was over they left without incident, and Antoine seemed to be relieved, and never brought up the subject again.

All of a sudden, new incidences occurred at the castle, and this time Eric was targeted. Someone was up to dirty tricks again. Antoine had been over to the castle while Eric was out, after he had arranged for a bomb to be planted in the winery that would trigger off an explosion, but he ensured that no one would suspect him, so from the moment he arrived at the castle he chatted with his mum, until he finally left. Angelique had seen him from her bedroom window, and would need to vow that he had not left his mother's side.

He greeted his mum with a kiss and told her that he would see her in a few days. When he got home he couldn't believe what he saw. He had arrived just in time to watch his home go up in smoke. Antoine was furious – this was supposed to be happening to his brother's winery and not his home, so he reached for his mobile phone and called Eric, who told him that they had also had a scare. They noticed a fire in the cave and managed to put it out, when they found a bomb that would have exploded in no time. Antoine found it rather intriguing that the bomb did not go off as planned; no one would have been injured, but Eric would be heartbroken to have had lost a fortune in *grand cru*. There were very matured bottles of Rothschild's wine in the winery and Eric had just drawn up an order with a chain of hotels he was to sell to.

Antoine was furious and he had some serious thinking to do. He needed to instruct the guys to do their jobs correctly. For the moment his only preoccupation was about who would have wanted to burn down his home. At that instant Indra came rushing down the road. When she saw the house completely destroyed she took her husband in her arms and tried to pacify him, while he cried like an infant. Eric arrived sometime later, and was really heartbroken for them. He knew how much Antoine loved the place, and that he was very attached to his home – for once, this was where he lived permanently. Eric had brought along the keys of Twin Pads in Calicorne. The tenants had emigrated to Australia, so the house was vacant.

Indra was quite happy to be close to where her sister lived. She placed Antonio and Anne in the private school at Calicorne, while Antoine was having a hard time to accept living in his brother's house. He hated being there, and he didn't like Mrs Verité. Antoine often thought how unfortunate he had been lately. Every time he tried something, everything just seemed to work against him. He waited for a while and then tried something different. It needed to be something that both Eric and Angelique cherished, something he could take away from them. Angelique hurt him, so he was going to hurt everyone close to her, including herself. He arranged for his men to enter the castle, while the family was over at Mountain's Peak. He called the men and gave them a date and time to remove the paintings and antiques. Everything was perfectly planned: they were to remove each article and replace it with replicas. Once again, things didn't work out as he had planned.

Eric called Antoine and told him that they weren't going to Mountain's Peak for another two days, and he needed to see him urgently. When Antoine arrived, Mrs Lemoin made a point of asking him and Indra to join them on their vacation to Mountain's Peak. At first he told them that he had some business to settle, but then he realised that it was a great idea to go along with them, so they wouldn't know that he had anything to do with the replacement of the antiques, so he agreed. He wasted no more time, and left immediately thereafter under the pretext that he was going to pack his bags and that he would meet them at the airport. As soon as he got into his car he called the boys and told them that he was going to be out of town, and that they were to carry out the job within three days, but he spoke in code language, so that Indra didn't understand.

Indra was all excited, because this was only her third time at Mountain's Peak, and she was looking forward to it. They spent exactly three weeks in the mountains and then headed for home. Everyone was to go straight to the castle and then leave the following morning. They finally arrived at the castle and dinner was being served. Mrs Verité and her husband were present as well, as they had been invited to spend their vacation with the Lemoin family.

Luther informed Eric about what had happened when they were away. He told Eric that something strange had occurred at the castle while they were away. They were minding the castle when strange men entered the premises and sprayed a substance into the air, and they all passed out. When they recovered, there was no trace of the guys. He called the police and nothing seemed to have been stolen.

So Eric just grinned and said, 'That is why one can never be too careful, it helps to take precautions, he said.'

Franco asked Eric if he could see the paintings. He really loved old paintings and had an antique shop in Calicorne, so Eric, joined by Antoine and Giovanni, did a little tour of the castle. Franco was an expert in telling the difference between originals and copies, and the first thing he noticed was that the paintings were copies. Antoine looked as if he had stage fright, and looked at Eric to see the expression on his face. He was expecting Eric to realise that the castle had been stripped of antiques that had been there for generations.

Antoine said, 'Oh my God! What a shame, so those guys actually stole all the family treasures. The bastards got away with it, you've got to call the police.'

Giovanni and Eric laughed, and told him that it wasn't necessary. If they managed such a trick, they would be most disappointed to find out that they had exchanged copies for copies. Giovanni looked at the disappointed grin on Antoine's face and giggled and then excused himself from the company, while Antoine pretended to be relieved, but he wanted to know where the originals were.

Eric was very evasive and just told him not to worry, that no one could get their hands on the treasure. Antoine didn't insist, because he didn't want them to guess that he was involved. The guys were well paid, and he still had a final payment due to them, and he was totally furious that it had cost him so much for a complete failure.

Indra was seeing a lot of Pedro, and Antoine did not trust his wife anymore; but she didn't trust him either, so she had him watched by a private eye. For months he was being followed, and she had learnt quite a good deal about Antoine and the people he was involved with, while he was having a difficult time trying to find evidence that she was having an affair with Pedro. Antoine thought differently, but what he did not know was that Indra had been having him followed for a very long time now, and she discovered that he was out to ruin and hurt Angelique and Eric because Angelique had taken away his manhood, and that was something he could never forgive her for.

Indra had become acquainted with some of Antoine's scumbag friends, and she used them to furnish her with information. Indra took full advantage of getting Angelique to speak to her about all the negative things that had happened since she was a teenager. Angelique didn't hesitate, knowing that it would do her good to try and understand certain things. Angelique told Indra how happy she had been, having Murielle as her best friend, and a wonderful fiancé she trusted with her whole life, but her fiancé had gone off with her best friend without warning, and as usual she was the last person to be informed about what had happened. There were months of bitterness until the storm was over. Indra wanted to understand why these things had happened. Indra asked Angelique to tell her about it; she told Angelique that her sister had turned out to be a monster, from the sweet little girl she used to be, and it was frightful to believe that Murielle could have changed so drastically. She needed to know why Murielle maintained that she was innocent, even after all the years she had spent in prison.

Then Angelique started off with the blackmailing of Mr Fourbourg, who eventually managed to get what he had always wanted from the word go, using Eric and Murielle to obtain it. Something went wrong and Mr Fourbourg was caught in the act. He had even gone so far as to include the murder of Mr Durand to make it look as if Alex was guilty. It was pathetic to see to what lengths these people were willing to go to obtain something. He paid for his crimes by going to jail for years on end, but still ended up recovering what he had been after in the first place. It was clear that he was out to destroy the Lemoin family. Angelique told Indra that she was sorry, but she felt that while he was jailed he still carried on behind bars. It certainly seemed that way then. Everything he told Murielle to do, she did without hesitation. That was very hard to swallow. She had changed from a best friend to the worst enemy one could imagine, and she made no secret about it. When Eric wanted out of the marriage, which had been a marriage of convenience in the first place, she refused to let go, under the pretext that she had fallen in love with him, knowing that he loved Angelique.

Angelique had no doubt about Eric's feeling towards her after the situation had been clarified and he had asked her to marry him. She didn't hesitate because she loved him just as much, and she most certainly wasn't going to step aside for a so-called friend who pretended to care for her, while she was simply using her to get Eric's favours. Angelique told Indra that it was the hardest blow of all when she found out that Murielle had actually tried to entice Eric to go to bed with her.

She spoke about how Antoine had been in love with her since they were teenagers, but that she loved him as a brother and he was hurt when she started seeing Eric. Somehow he accepted the fact only because he was fighting a losing battle and had to step down. He couldn't bear a grudge for eternity so he gave them his blessings and ever since he had turned out to be extremely understanding and really gave them a helping hand. Then the children were born, and Antoine proved his sincerity by being present and helpful in every possible way concerning them and was really great.

Then there were the incidents of the birthday presents the twins had received on every birthday since they were born, They had never found out who the anonymous person was, and the presents had never stopped. The presents were always exceptional and always turned out to be something the kids desired and cherished, but most of the time it was somewhat dangerous, and very often harmed the children. The person who sent the presents wanted to harm Angelo – there was no doubt about that. They found out much later, because Anemone always had safe toys and harmless presents, while Angelo got planes that blew up in his face and so on. Then came the chocolates. Once again the harm was intended for Angelo, but came off on Anemone instead, because she had opened up her brother's Easter egg instead of her own, and she would have died had she eaten a little more. No one even knew that she had eaten the chocolate bunny, because she had so much chocolate at that time. A few months later Angelo had died because they were negligent in finding what the original cause of Anemone's poisoning was. They looked around and found the video that Antoine had made the day before Angelo died and they played it and it brought back fond memories. They had this great video of the whole family before Angelo died. No one was absent, as if it was planned in advance but how could it have been, when everyone turned up by pure coincidence because they were only supposed to meet later that afternoon? After Angelo's autopsy showed that he was poisoned, it was really scary. And they started having doubts, until it was proven that Murielle had planned Angelo's death.

Indra knew that Murielle was implicated in the matter, but she did not understand why she would have wanted to kill an innocent little boy of six years old, and not Angelique or Eric, whom she hated. If Murielle wanted to get back at Eric and Angelique, she could have used a different tactic, and it could have been someone else who was responsible, but who? Mr Fourbourg and Murielle were the only two people who had an ulterior motive for carrying out a killing of such a kind, because she had made threats and seemed to have carried them out, until she too got caught and went to jail, and tried to baffle everyone by insisting that she was innocent – but the proof showed that she was guilty.

Angelique was reliving every moment as she told Indra her story and it was clear that it was very painful for her, but it helped her, to try to understand and get some peace of mind. Indra told her that they would talk again, and that it was good getting things off her chest, and if she felt that she needed someone to talk to, she could just ring her and she would come right over.

Indra went home and spoke to Antoine, who was brooding in his corner as usual. She told him that she had spoken to Angelique, and from what she gathered, they were very close once upon a time, and she couldn't understand why he was making her pay for not wanting him, and it was certainly not necessary to have taken it out on Anemone. Antoine told Indra that these were delicate matters and did not concern her at all. He told her that she needed to stop seeing Pedro before he caused trouble. Indra didn't like his tone of voice, and she wasn't going to be threatened by Antoine, so she told him to mind his P's and Q's and not to threaten her, because she was ready to walk out of the marriage, as easily as she had walked into it. She also threatened to take her children along with her, knowing that he would never part with his son. Antoine knew that she was serious about leaving him, and that was the last thing he wanted right now; he needed her, so he tried to calm her down, and asked her to forgive him. Indra accepted his apology and told him that she had some things to settle with Murielle and that he was not to wait up for her.

Indra found Murielle at home and told her why she had come to visit coming right to the point. She told Murielle that a lot had been going on in Angelique's life and she needed to understand why she had been pretending to be Angelique's friend when all she wanted was Eric, and why she had been lying about not having anything to do with Angelo's death when everything proved her guilty. She said it was no longer necessary because she had gone to prison for her crimes and paid her debt to society. Indra told her that it was very bad to keep ongoing hatred that caused so many people's deaths.

Murielle told Indra that she was very disappointed that she didn't have enough faith in her to believe that she was innocent and insisted that she couldn't even imagine doing something so cruel, and that she was being sincere when she said that she had absolutely nothing to do with any of the murders – she was no murderer. As for Angelique, she was a good friend once upon a time, but it was true that she fell in love with Eric and jumped at the opportunity her father gave her when he was blackmailing the Lemoin family, and that was why she held on to Eric, knowing that if she let him out of her sight, he would go straight back into the arms of Angelique.

Indra listened attentively and tried very hard to believe her sister, but there was still something odd about how she unfolded the tale. It was possible that she didn't participate in all the crimes, but she certainly had a lot to do with it. Knowing her father, he was not going to let anyone off the hook. Indra had thanked Murielle for talking to her and left, promising to be back soon.

Some time later Indra went and spoke to her father, who didn't deny having blackmailed Alex, because Alex never gave what was due to him, so he wanted to teach him a lesson and he got caught in the pleasure of seeing Alex beg for mercy. He never regretted having done what he did, because for once he was in full power, and he got so carried away that it didn't make a difference who got hurt in the process. Indra asked him why he had forced Eric to marry Murielle, knowing that it wouldn't last for ever? He told her that he had overheard her speaking to Tina about how much she loved Eric, and that she didn't want to hurt Angelique, but she was going to make a move anyway. So he stopped her and told her that he had a better idea, and she liked it.

He had also done fraudulent things from his prison cell, and gave Murielle orders to carry out, which she did without hesitation for the love of Eric. She had also written threatening notes to them and organised some dirty tricks, but never went as far as killing people. Mr Durand's death was an accident, but there was nothing he could do to cover it up.

Indra went about doing her investigations, as if she were a cop, and really got into being a Sherlock Holmes detective; she started liking what she was doing. Some time later she spent a day with Angelique and they continued their conversation from where they had left off some time back and Indra told her what she had found out from Murielle and her father, trying to make sense of the whole thing. Angelique told her about the incidents that occurred in between. There were all those incidents of the dogs being poisoned and strangled, and always with a blue ribbon, which proved once again that someone was out to hurt Angelo, because the dog was his present.

Then there was the school incident where a man offered a tattoo to Angelo and refused to give one to Anemone as well. Angelo's little friends also got some innocent tattoos and nothing happened to them. Angelo was completely drugged by the time he got home, and he needed to be taken to the hospital where they found that the dose was enough for him to become addicted if he carried on having it, and that was their intention because he had been approached another time, and asked if he wanted a tattoo, but he screamed for help and the man disappeared. And then there was the incident at the kindergarten with the Polish tutor who handed out the golden sherbet packet he had won as a king, while all the other children got red sherbet packets. The lady who had given them the sherbet never tried to hide her identity, and when the person who had hired her found out, she was brutally murdered, maybe because she threatened to talk.

Then suddenly Eric's life was in danger. Someone had tried to run him down on several occasions. They even followed him to his jogging area, where he came close to death more than once. They had tried to electrocute him, killing a young man in his early twenties instead, and had sent him death-threatening notes, and even tampered with his car's brakes.

Indra went about doing her homework, and she decided that if Murielle wanted to hurt Eric, there was one way she could get through to him, because everybody knew that Angelo was the apple of his eye, and he was very close to him. So she decided that Angelo was a good target, knowing that Angelique might not be able to have another son thereafter and Eric would become frustrated. But when she didn't succeed in killing Angelo the first time why did she continue with him, when she could have targeted someone else in the family such as Angelique, or Eric himself? Perhaps she still had hope of capturing Eric's heart and there was only one way of doing that and it was by getting rid of Angelique herself.

Indra had even asked Mrs Verité about what had happened and what she thought about the whole set-up. Then again, there were the two sons of Mrs Verité who purposely poisoned one of the dogs because he never stopped barking. Did they have something against the Lemoins to try and drug their boy knowing that the little girl wouldn't do? Nothing was impossible from drug addicts. Maybe they were threatening Angelo because he had seen where they stashed their drugs, and like any other little boy he mounted his curiosity and made them angry, so they must have bribed him to keep quite, while they tried to get rid of him at the same time. They were totally out of it and sick in their heads; they were capable of anything, and, after all, they disappeared shortly thereafter.

Here she was trying to find a solution to all the problems, but everything kept on bringing her back to her father and Murielle. Not forgetting Mrs Verité who often made home-made sweets and cakes for the children, but she sounded rather innocent. Now Indra had her suspects, and her sister still seemed to be number one, followed by Jason and Keanan Verité, but she wasn't going to leave out her father – he was not totally innocent either.

Indra was happy with all the material she had put together; now all she needed was to solve the puzzle, but there were too many missing pieces, and she was going to find them. Her findings turned out to be amazing and outstanding. The more she got into it, she understood that the planning was a man's job and it sounded more like a man's job, because it took a lot of knowledge to know where to find the lowest scumbags possible and the right people to hire for the jobs. One needed to be sure that they would not retaliate if they were caught, and that they would never mention who the person was who hired them in the first place. In Murielle's case it seemed as though she had not chosen them carefully enough, because they always admitted that she had hired them, unless of course she was really framed. The person would have had to deal with cold-blooded murderers and have a lot of money to pay them off, and keep them quiet if they were caught, and once again it didn't make sense, because Murielle didn't have a dime, let alone a fortune, unless she had been using Paolo's money.

Indra had decided to go over the material she already had and compare it to her new findings. She studied every possibility and concluded that Murielle could never have planned everything on her own; she would have needed an expert as an accomplice, and it had to be someone she knew mighty well. The person involved would need to have been criminally related in the past and know really bad criminals, and have a hell of a lot of money too, because she didn't have any and it was evident that the accomplice was paying for her.

Indra had put two and two together and found that the only person she could lean on was Paolo, who had a great deal of money, but as for knowing scumbag people, that was another matter, because Paolo came from a Christian family. However, didn't change the fact that his family was originally from Sicily and there was certainly some Mafia business going on there. The more Indra got into it the more fulfilled she felt, and she got closer and closer by the day. After several sessions with Murielle she started having doubts, because Murielle still wanted her name to be cleared and wanted to prove her innocence.

A month later they were having a barbecue at the castle when the telephone rang, and the gentleman on the other line wanted to speak to Edwina. She excused herself from the company and shortly thereafter had yet another heart attack, and they needed to get her to a hospital. Angelique tried to find out what the call was about, and who the caller was, but Edwina refused to tell her, and Angelique left it at that, knowing that the tiniest worry could trigger off a fatal heart attack. Edwina was admitted to the hospital, where she stayed for a few weeks, and still refused to tell them who had called that day.

In the meantime, Indra was making headway with her investigations and sometimes went to see Mrs Lemoin and asked her opinion about things, but Mrs Lemoin told her that those things were for others to discover, and that it was all just too sad and she didn't want to think about it anymore, and preferred to change the subject, and Indra respected her wishes.

Then Indra remembered that Antoine had also been attacked on numerous occasions; for example, when they had connected all his electrical appliances in his home and left the water to run from the taps, there was no doubt that someone was trying to electrocute him, and someone had tried to run him over as well.

Coming back to Angelique, it appeared that she was the only person who was not targeted; nothing ever happened to her, and it seemed as if they were out to get only the males in the Lemoin family. She remembered the incident when Pedro called her about the bomb at Alex's house, and that Paolo had alerted him; that was some way of trying to get out of the circle – by informing the people concerned – but then why would he want to be noticed if he had something to do with it?

When they stripped all Alex's cars he cherished, and still showed up for the rally, it was obvious because they thought that if they came along no one would suspect them; but what they didn't know, was that a private detective had been following them for some time, but even the photos turned out to be false for some reason or another. Something that was even more intriguing, was about who had suddenly had the bright idea of hiring a private eye at that specific time, and why not before? And because of that, a third person was killed.

Even after Mr Lemoin had died and they lived at the castle, the game still continued. Murielle went to jail for the second time, and managed to get herself in trouble even from behind bars. When the triplets were abducted from the clinic, she once again denied the accusation, but was found guilty because it was proven that they were inmates. She insisted that she was innocent.

They had exactly the same method of payment: at first, she would give them a key and an advance of money, and when the job was done, she got in contact with them by telephone, and gave them instructions to go to a locker at the station where they removed the note therein with another key and a code; they would take it to the airport where they were to find the rest of their payments. There was something very peculiar about something of vital importance that none of the investigators or even the private detectives had found out. Who did the safe belong to? There were hidden cameras planted in the alleys and everywhere close to the safe lockers, and they would surely have seen the person who deposited the money, but it seemed that the majority of the investigators were being bribed as well.

Both Murielle and Paolo had moved to Brazil, after Mr Lemoin died, for which they took the blame. Murielle especially needed to get away, and that is where they stayed for quite a few years, and it didn't stop incidents occurring.

If they were managing to get things done all the way from Brazil, they were certainly professionals in this field and had powerful people to pull the strings. They had wiped out Angelo and Alex, another innocent man got killed in Eric's place and a woman was murdered because she knew too much; they didn't know about the unaccounted-for ones – the death toll could be much higher for all they knew.

They continued to strike out to Eric, but just couldn't get him down, so they tried to kill Leonardo and Angelo, and they had almost succeeded with Angelo, but Leonardo was a very clever boy and made the assailant feel like an amateur, which he wasn't. Angelique's two younger boys were well aware that someone was out to harm them and they kept clear of traps. When Angelo almost drowned, after he had been pushed into a dam of water and was left with a memory loss, they couldn't have known that Leonardo had taken up life-saving lessons that saved his own life and that of his brother. But it didn't stop there. It continued with Anemone. No one wanted to harm Anemone, but they managed to kill her future husband and attempted to kill Giovanni on several occasions as well. They even managed to murder Marc's parents. Why would Murielle want to go so far? Marc was no concern of hers; she had Eric and Angelique to deal with. Beyond that it made no sense.

Indra had turned into a real Sherlock Holmes. She was keeping a watchful eye on all the parties concerned when strange things started happening to Antoine. He started receiving presents in the post and they were obviously from an anonymous person, because there were never any cards or messages either, Antoine was rather worried and thought that he would mention this to Indra. On another occasion, his car had a brake failure and he managed to steer clear of a fatal accident – he lost two of his fingers though. As usual, the only thing they could do was report it to the police and see what they could turn up. In the meantime he felt as if he was going mad, and that he was imagining things. Sometimes he would see things that had occurred a long time ago and it looked so real it was as if history were repeating itself, and he was very worried indeed. Someone was trying to make him go off his rocker, and was succeeding, because it drove him nuts, and he became very edgy with nerves, and he worried for his children.

One day while he went to the cave to get some wine, while Indra was out, he got locked into the cellar and was left there for a night and a day, without anything to eat, and it was freezing cold. At the time Antoine went in to the cellar he was alone at home; Indra was out shopping with Murielle, and there must have been someone else in his home at that time, because they deliberately locked the wine cellar's door behind him. When Indra got back from her shopping spree, the doors were wide open as she had left it before she left, and Antoine was nowhere in sight. She waited for a couple of hours, and he still hadn't got back home. It sometimes happened that he just went off and reappeared the next morning, so she didn't worry too much.

When he'd been gone for over twenty-four hours, she thought that it was better to report him missing. They searched all round the house, thinking that he might have fallen and passed out somewhere; then they decided to look in the cellar, but the door was locked and there was no key in the door, so they knocked and heard him making sounds. Indra immediately got the spare keys and got him out; he was in a state, and snapped at everyone for leaving him in there.

Antoine considered himself lucky that they had found him before he froze and starved to death, because Indra never went into the cave. He could have rotted in there. When he had recovered from the shock he organised a fishing trip with the children and Indra. So they went to a private fishing area where the children could play. Antoine felt like swimming in the river. All of a sudden, Indra noticed that he was going down, and had a hard time to come back to the surface; it seemed as if he were being pulled from down under, but there was nothing she could do but run for help. There weren't many people in sight so she needed to go a little bit further where she found some campers who she called for help and some men came running and dived in to save him.

Antoine insisted that someone had been trying to pull him down so that he would drown, but there were no signs of divers in the area because it was prohibited, so they told him that he had probably trodden on some weeds and got his feet tangled in them. Antoine felt as if he were going mad, and he was on the verge of having a nervous breakdown when Indra suggested that he go on a long holiday to change his mind about everything. He needed to go abroad for a few weeks, to get everything off his chest. He agreed, only because he felt that he was going insane, but he wanted her to come along. She told him that he needed the break and it would do him good to go on his own. He decided that he would go to an island, so he chose the Maldives and boarded a plane the very next day.

While Antoine was away, Indra saw a lot of Angelique, and life seemed to be treating her well. It had done her the world of good to speak to Indra about all the things that bothered her, and she thought that she should have had therapy a long time ago. Indra really had got her out of the mess she was in mentally.

Antoine had scarcely been gone for two weeks when they received a call from the emergency services asking them to meet him at the airport with an ambulance.

Antoine had been beaten up by some girl's boyfriend, who was now in custody. It appeared that Antoine touched the girl where he shouldn't have, and her boyfriend freaked out and broke his nose and cracked his jawbone as well. The man was arrested and Antoine was taken to hospital and then deported immediately after the incident. They didn't tolerate such behaviour in Maldives.

Antoine had hardly recovered when he began being blackmailed about an incident that had occurred many years previously. He was told that if he didn't pay in lump sums he would have to pay the price with death, and they threatened to kill his son too if he didn't pay up rapidly. Antoine became scared and kept on paying, and he really started feeling the weight of the loss of the money from his account. He never told Indra about it either, until they ran into severe financial problems. Antoine's millions had been wiped out since the company went down the drain, and now he had to use his percentage of the winery and the income of the apartment building he was renting out.

Antoine never stopped blaming Angelique for all the misfortune that fell upon him and his family, and he wanted her to pay. Up until now she seemed to be getting off quite freely, while he suffered the consequences, but this time he wanted to do something that would shut her up for good. Angelique went shopping every Thursday at ten in the morning so that she could be back with fresh food for the children when they got back from school. One Thursday she went to the supermarket, after Indra had arranged a rendezvous with her at nine forty-five. They shopped and conversed, when suddenly a man came along and tried to trip Angelique, causing her to fall, and he held a spray can in his hand and was going to spray the contents into her face when Indra looked up and recognised Jack. Angelique hadn't seen what Jack's intentions were at that moment, but Indra winked an eye and he knew that she had recognised him. Jack excused himself and Indra introduced him to Angelique as a personal friend. After that, they invited Jack to have a cup of coffee with them. When Angelique decided that she had to leave before the boys got home, Indra told her to go along and that she would see her later. Indra stayed with Jack, and told him that she was aware of Antoine's schemes, and she would appreciate it if no harm came to Angelique. Indra told Jack that she would double the amount offered if he didn't do anything else for Antoine. Jack promised that he would do no more jobs for Antoine, and he kept his word.

Indra left things at that, until the next incident, which proved that her husband was going insane. He had organised someone else to rape Angelique again, only this time the man was to finish her off by disfiguring her face with caustic soda and leave her to suffer. The man had been well informed of where he would find Angelique – at the women's club hall. Angelique was always the first to arrive because she had the keys to the hall and everybody else generally arrived thirty minutes later. But this time the man was out of luck.

Angelique was to be raped in the recreation centre and the rapist was supposed to pull her to a safe haven when she had been totally knocked out, where he was supposed to pour the caustic soda over her face. But the man wasn't lucky enough to get as far as doing what he intended to, because what he didn't know was that Angelique had been warned in advance, and the ladies were on the scene, but stayed out of sight so they couldn't be seen. They needed to catch him red-handed and give him the hiding of his life and then have him arrested.

When she arrived at the recreation centre where they were preparing for a masked ball, Angelique knew that her assailant was in the hall already, but he didn't know that everybody else was there too. And he didn't waste any time.

She had scarcely put her head through the door and he had already pulled off her clothes, but she was ready for him. She kicked him in the groin about three times until he fell down in pain. She had got hold of a stick and beat the man to a pulp; she just continued until the ladies stopped her. When they wanted to tie him up they felt his pulse, but the man wasn't breathing anymore. Angelique had killed her assailant, and she felt terrible, but there was no doubt that he would have killed her; when the police had taken away his body they found a note in his pocket, giving him specific instructions; they had also found the caustic soda. Angelique knew that Antoine was behind all of it and because of him another man had died, for a measly amount of money.

Antoine's life became a misery, and Indra could not bear to see him that way. He was aggressive, and had a bad influence on the children, so she decided to leave him. He begged her to stay with him, but she refused. She told him that she couldn't live with a murderer, and that she knew about his scams to destroy Angelique, and she wasn't going to stay and watch people who loved one another destroy each other, it was too hard, and he was sick and needed treatment. He had gone too far, he had ruined his own life and that of his family. They had a big battle, and finally custody of the children was awarded to Indra. She had moved far away from him, leaving him rock bottom. Indra knew how much he loved and adored his son, but she was being strict, and only allowed him to see Antonio twice a month, and he thought that she was being cruel, but she soon reminded him who the cruel being was.

Antoine thought that he would teach her a lesson for not allowing him to see Antonio. Already he was not allowed to see Romeo, so he became desperate, and sought revenge by kidnapping Antonio and leaving the country. Indra was sick with worry. She reported it to the police and it took a week before they realised that he had left the country, and another to find which country he had gone to. They had found Antoine and Antonio, on a yacht on the Mediterranean and immediately arrested him for abduction.

Indra had her fair share of Antoine's tantrums and she needed to do something, but Mrs Lemoin and Eric managed to get him out of prison in no time. He pursued Indra, and tried to bring about a reconciliation with her, but she refused and told him that he was too cruel, and that she didn't want to see him anymore. She told him of her intentions to marry Pedro in the very near future, and she didn't want him to get in the way, otherwise he might regret it. Antoine was insanely jealous after he heard that they had got married and that Indra was expecting Pedro's child. He felt like killing the guy. There was no way that his son was going to live with a stepfather. He just couldn't accept that.

Antoine started to neglect himself: he never shaved and he wore creased clothes and drank from morning till night. He looked like a real vagabond and his children no longer recognised him. He was very untidy and a drunken bum. Everybody avoided him like the plague. He sometimes drove up to the castle as drunk as a lord, insisting to see Romeo, and when he wasn't allowed to, he would insult everyone, including his mum, who was just about the only person who had compassion for her son. Edwina would scold him and tell him to pull himself together, but he was rebellious and did his own thing.

Angelique and Anemone still had a problem staying under the same roof as Antoine and made it clear that they would leave every time he needed to stay over. Edwina knew that Antoine was no angel, but she couldn't understand why Angelique and Anemone rejected Antoine; it had been putting a strain on the family. Angelique told her mother-in-law that she wasn't to worry about it, it was to teach him a lesson; he needed to be ignored and not pampered – the latter would just make him worst. Edwina knew that there was much more to it than met the eye, and she knew that she wasn't going to get it from any of her family, so she decided to find out by herself. She also knew powerful people.

Antoine left, and tried to pull himself together, and succeeded to look decent. For a little while he started looking like a gentleman. He had sold his apartment buildings and got a big sum of money from the sale, but he had to be careful not to overspend, because his financial standing was disastrous; he had only one asset to his name and that was Mountain's Peak, and he couldn't part with it even if he had to starve to death, but he knew that his family would help him out if need be – after all, he did have a share in the winery.

Antoine worked and was still living in Eric's home in Calicorne and he did what was expected of him on his visits to the children, although the fact of seeing Indra and Pedro happy made him want to puke; but he was in no position to overpower them. He went back to drinking and gambling; he spent his nights in pubs and entertained hookers all the time, until he was rock bottom again, only this time he was left penniless, because of his own carelessness, and he had to call on Eric for help, knowing that he would never leave him in the lurch.

Antoine's mum found out all the bad things that Antoine got up to, but she still loved her son, and was prepared to do anything to ease his pain. She had spoken to Indra about visits to the children, because Indra refused to have him visiting or minding the children without the assistance of a social worker, because she didn't trust him. She felt that he was unreliable, and in some way a danger. After a lot of consideration, Indra adhered to Mrs Lemoin's request, only because she had a lot of respect for her ex-mother-in-law, and knew that she didn't have long to live. Because of Mrs Lemoin she allowed him to have the children every weekend for a while, until he showed signs of talking Antonio into going on a fishing trip for a weekend. Indra had warned them not to go any further than his house and malls, and that if they thought he was misleading them they were to run into the nearest shop and hide from him, and then call her. About a month later that was exactly what happened, and this time Indra got a court order, that he was not to see the children for more than an hour in a social worker's presence at all times. He had brought it upon himself and she wasn't going to change her mind.

A few months later, Mrs Lemoin died, and on her deathbed she told Angelique that she had left a letter for her and that she was sorry for all the pain Antoine had caused her, and that she was terribly brave. It was the most courageous thing anyone could do, to keep such painful and terrible secrets simply because she didn't want to make others suffer, but it was time for her to bring everything into the open as soon as possible and she would have peace of mind thereafter.

Angelique read the letter that Edwina had left, in which she admitted being aware of everything that Antoine had done to her and her family from beginning to end. At first it was hard to believe, but she understood that Antoine had become a monster. She promised that if she had known before, she would have done something about it, but unfortunately she had only known for few weeks. After Angelique had read the letter to Indra, Indra told her that she too had a confession to make, and that what she had to say had better be done when the whole family was present, and that it was the perfect time to do so, because she had spoken to Mrs Lemoin before she died and she wanted it that way.

They called a meeting and invited Murielle, Mr Fourbourg, Paolo, Pedro, Mr and Mrs Mancheta and everybody else concerned. At first Eric refused to have all those people at his mother's funeral, but Angelique and Giovanni convinced him that it was necessary. He couldn't think of anything that concerned them, but gave in eventually and accepted.

When everyone was seated, Antoine sat beside his brother, while everybody else sat on the opposite side from them. Indra had called for everyone's attention, when Antoine complained about having to listen to her, because she was no longer part of the family, and it wasn't out of respect that she was there but out of sheer selfishness, in the presence of her new family, after all the humiliation she had caused him. He didn't want her to make a speech and Eric agreed with Antoine, but Indra insisted that it was of the utmost importance that they listen to what she had to say and then decide whether it was worthwhile or not.

Indra started by saying, 'I stand accused of doing some unscrupulous things myself but I am proud to say, my idea paid off, otherwise you all might have continued to believe a sob story for the rest of your lives; but I cannot allow innocent people to be regarded as guilty, when the only thing they stand guilty of is being framed. I have valid reason to clarify the situation right now.

'I'll start with myself. When I married Antoine, I knew that he was in love with Angelique and just about getting over it, or so I thought at the time. I had always cared about Antoine since I was a teenager, but he only had eyes for Angelique, so I called it a day until he popped the question, and then I did it out of love, knowing that he was unable to have children of his own, and I didn't regret having done so, because he turned out to be a wonderful husband.

'A short while later, I started having doubts about Antoine's feelings towards me, because he praised everything Angelique did, and constantly compared me to her. Then he suddenly directed his love towards Anemone, and that was innocent, so I was proud of him, but the jealousy started after Romeo's birth, when he played an exaggerated role in the child's upbringing. I tolerated it because I knew how he felt about children, and I really wished that we had children of our own. I often saw videos of him playing with his nephews and nieces, and it was clear to see that he loved Angelique from the word go.

'It all started the day that Angelique and Giovanni called at our home and severed Antoine's groin. I was horrified when he refused to have them arrested for the barbaric act, and made everyone believe that he had been done in by a teenager, who mistook him for someone else. I didn't like the lie, but he pleaded with me to keep it to my self for a while, but I needed to know more because he wouldn't tell me anything, so I spoke to Angelique.

'Since that day, Antoine worked out ways to make Angelique pay for taking away his pride, and he made no secret that he wanted her to pay dearly for taking his manhood. Antoine never told me what he intended to do, but I wasn't expecting anything brutal, until he found out who informed Angelique about Romeo being his son, and gave her the medical file as well. Antoine had paid a few guys to force Melany to invite Angelique, and they killed Melany and then raped Angelique. His intention was for Angelique to find the mutilated body when she looked for something to wear, because they had gone off with her clothes, leaving her disfigured and traumatised.'

Angelique had called Indra after she had recovered from her injuries, and asked her to keep an eye on Antoine, telling her about her suspicions that he had killed Melany. Indra didn't put it past him, because he kept repeating that

Angelique was going to suffer, and she knew that it was one of Antoine's plans to make her life a misery. Indra hired some of Antoine's own people to follow him around and tell her about his intentions, and when she thought that it was going too far, she started investigating herself.

She warned them that they were going to be totally shocked to hear that everything that happened to them had been planned by Antoine. It started with the embezzlement of money, being transferred in Eric's name into foreign currencies. Antoine was hoping that his father would see what a crook Eric was, but what he didn't intend was to get Mr Fourbourg to blackmail Alex. He left it at that when he saw that things were turning to his advantage.

Antoine would have done anything to hold on to Angelique, but he honestly didn't know anything about the wedding. Later it turned to his advantage that they walked into the so-called eloped couple's marriage, once again without intention. When he beat up his brother, it was not only out of anger for his marrying Murielle, but also because he wanted to do so, since Eric had captured Angelique's heart. It was a golden opportunity, and he used it well by staying with Angelique throughout her painstaking ordeal, while she was trying to recover from the shock that Eric had dumped her for her best friend Murielle.

Antoine panicked when he found out that Eric had annulled his marriage to Murielle, and asked Angelique to marry him. Antoine pretended to approve and was very happy for them, until the twins were born. He found a way of creeping into their hearts and spoiled them, and nothing was too good or expensive for these children. Antoine was jealous of his brother and hated him; he was ready to destroy anything that was dear to Eric's heart, so he thought of a plan.

He started off by sending anonymous presents in the post. No wonder it always turned out to be something the children needed. Then he started getting people to threaten Eric, and trying to run him over while he was walking or jogging; even the brake failure and the electrocution of the man in the gym cubicle was Antoine's way of trying to get him out of the way so that he could worm his way back into Angelique's life. When his plans were falling apart, he would buy animals for the children, and then have them poisoned and strangled.

Antoine noticed that not even the worst things were disturbing Angelique and Eric, so he had to find something radical. He was going to kill Angelo, not because he disliked the child, but because he was Eric's pride and joy; so he framed Murielle for the crime. Antoine had hired Fakhir and paid him a lot of money to lie about Murielle, but it was true that Fakhir didn't know what the powder contained when he carried out the job. Even after Fakhir had found out about Angelo's death, he played the game, because he had earned a fortune for framing Murielle, and he left the country thereafter with a comfortable amount of money. Some of the people who did the dirty jobs were well paid, and didn't mind going to jail, while he bought their silence.

Antoine's intentions were very clear: he specifically wrapped Anemone's packages in pink so that she didn't touch her brother's, but unfortunately she almost died because of that.

Then, later, he had the perfect opportunity, and he did it in style while Angelique was out doing her shopping. This time he was going to succeed and he called everyone to come round within an hour and told them that he had something to show them. He encouraged Angelo to eat his chocolate, while he opened a marshmallow for Anemone. They got dirty and he made a video tape, expecting everyone to turn up at any minute, so he managed to have the entire family on the video, the last day of Angelo's life. Antoine had killed Angelo.

He felt that he had achieved something, but decided that it wasn't enough. He found a scapegoat to take the rap for him, who went to prison because she was framed. Murielle spent years in jail for a murder she hadn't committed. When Grandma Lemoin died, he hated Eric all the more for inheriting the castle and all the businesses, but when he found out, that Angelique was pregnant again, he had to get someone to abduct the children, so he chose someone from the same prison as Murielle, and he was in luck, because he had her cell-mate. Like all the others, the method of payment was the same. Once again Murielle was framed, so she did a longer sentence than usual.

Murielle was just settling down, when he targeted again. He had heard that they'd been invited to a party, to which both himself and Indra were invited as well, so he got the guys to follow them and see that the road was blocked after midnight, meaning that they would have to drive past the Lemoins' premises, making them do a detour. When they were about five hundred metres from the premises, they were to use the remote control detonator and blow the house to cinders. He also knew that they would stop to see what happened, and then the detonator was to be planted in their car, so that they could be arrested when the police searched the cars. Antoine did it all to make Murielle suffer, because he had no one else to use and he wanted to blow his family home, knowing that Eric would probably inherit that too; he also knew how Eric felt about his father's cars, and how important it was for him to participate at every rally.

This time he was going to give them a big surprise. He heard that Paolo was a rally driver, and that he'd been enquiring about how he could be a pilot at that specific rally. Antoine immediately organised that the chairman hire Paolo as one of the drivers for one of his father's cars. He organised for the chairman to tell him that he had to visit the warehouse after twelve, and later called him back to tell him that he didn't have to do the visit after all, because the warehouse was being closed very early that evening, and Paolo obeyed. But Antoine, knowing that they had a private eye following Murielle and Paolo, hired someone else to follow them and snatch their bike and dress very similarly to them for at least an hour. He wasn't expecting it to work, but he had to try.

Antoine had given instructions to the private eye, and told him not to get too close to them, but he was to take photos of them wherever they went and then bring them to him the morning of the rally. Antoine was glad that the guys had done a thorough job, and no one knew that it was an inside scheme, but he hadn't anticipated his father dying, and he sincerely felt bad about it, but couldn't do anything.

When he saw that nothing was going to separate Angelique and Eric, he went away for a while, and then came back and started to spoil Leandra, Leonardo and Angelo, but he concentrated on Leonardo, for the specific reason that he had a lot in common with his dead brother Angelo and Eric protected him like a hawk. Everything seemed to be going too smoothly for his liking; he needed some action. Knowing that neither of the boys could swim, and that they liked going up to the water dams at least twice a week, he hired a man to look out for when the gardener was out of sight, to push the boys into the dam and leave them to drown, but what he didn't know was that Leonardo had been doing life-saving lessons and managed to save himself and his brother.

When he didn't succeed, he hired the same person who had pushed the boys into the dam, and had a spare key made for him to hide in the cave. If ever he were caught, he would have pretended that he wanted to steal a few bottles of wine because he was an alcoholic, which he was. He had boozed most of the time in the cave, until he finally got his awaited opportunity to knock Leonardo out cold and leave him to die in the attic where he couldn't reach the cellar. But he was too drunk and didn't knock the kid out enough to be badly injured and incapable of helping himself. The man had done what he was told to do and politely left from the same door he had come in, taking along with him a bottle of Rothschild, which he drank like ordinary wine. He also helped himself to cognac and calvados and left without a trace.

He married Indra to spite Eric, knowing that it would cause animosity between them, because of the friction between the two families. When Antoine had got used to married life, he no longer concentrated on destroying Eric personally, but he wanted to upset the apple-cart in his family.

When Anemone became a teenager, Antoine appreciated her asking his advice on certain things and he was very proud of her. He never intended to harm her or Leandra, nor even Angelique for that matter. He completely took his attention from Angelique and directed it towards Anemone. He interfered in her private life, and even told her who she was supposed to date. There was no doubt that he disliked Marc du Preez. There was something strange though, he took an instant liking to Giovanni Mancheta, for some unknown reason, but what he didn't know, was that Anemone was already falling in love with Giovanni at the time.

Antoine was out of his mind, and ready for anything that got in his way. Indra also told them about the blue room she had found recently. Indra came across a secret blue room where Antoine developed nude photos, and the walls were infested with pictures of Angelique, from when she was a teenager, and of Anemone as well; he even had video pictures. This must have been going on for an eternity, and no one ever found out.

When Anemone invited him and Indra to her graduation party, he was very excited and had the perfect opportunity to carry out his plans. He had drugged Indra, and made sure that she was asleep, before tiptoeing into Anemone's bedroom. He drugged both Marc and Anemone before going to bed, and, sexually abusing Anemone, took her virginity, not knowing that he had recovered from his sterility until he heard that Anemone was pregnant. He had spoken to Marc and knew they weren't having a sexual relationship, and as far as he was concerned it was the first time, at the party. Antoine went and got himself tested, and found that he could finally have children of his own.

When Indra and Antoine had their first child, it was no miracle. Antoine had known for years that he was no longer sterile. From the very start, Antoine's intentions were to get rid of Marc, who was blamed for making Anemone pregnant, and he wasn't going to allow his son to call another man 'daddy'. So he carried out his plans as usual, when he understood that Marc was going abroad to study. He put his plans on hold and was content with his role as godfather, so Marc was no threat at that time. Antoine's attitude changed when Marc came home for a few months to get to know his so-called son. And finally wedding bells were ringing, and Antoine wanted to make sure that Marc wasn't going to hear them, Antoine had become very close to Giovanni, and used him as a scapegoat, knowing that Giovanni loved Anemone, and that he didn't like Marc.

He organised someone to plant the bomb in Marc's car, after they had concluded the meeting where everyone agreed that Marc was to drive up to Marula to see the medical centre before the wedding. That was Antoine's idea, but Eric had a better idea. He suggested that they go and pick him up, and blindfold him throughout the journey. This time Antoine's plan didn't work, but he knew that sometime or the other, Marc needed to drive his car; otherwise he had a lot more up his sleeve anyway. But he had already thought of another plan, that all the guys who were invited to the bachelor's party were to meet at the castle, where he offered them a drink before they left. He saw the hairdryer on the dresser a while before, and got one of the guys to remove it and leave straightaway, after he had told them to work out a plan.

At the party Marc got very drunk, and Antoine seemed to be encouraging him to get tipsy. People were going to and fro into the bathroom at regular intervals, so no one could tell exactly how and who had tampered with the wiring of the dryer. They also purposely loosened the cupboard, so that if someone just reached to get a toothbrush or something, it would come crumbling down. Antoine was not at all sure that the electrocution would take place, so he actually ensured that there were some hijackers to keep an eye on the Cadillac that was supposed to have brought him to the church. They would have shot Marc, with a silencer on the gun, and left the chauffeur and Xavier to go free and it would have looked as if Giovanni had planned it.

When Anemone married Giovanni, he gave them their blessings, but he didn't like the way Romeo adored Giovanni, so they had lots of arguments, but Antoine also knew that Giovanni had a lot of sympathy for him because he couldn't have children of his own. Then Marc's family got in the way: they threatened to adopt Romeo, who wasn't even family of theirs. They never knew, and never would, because Antoine shut them up for good, and made it look like a break-in.

When Romeo got sick, he knew that someday or the other the truth would eventually be found out, but he had so much unfinished business to see to, and it was essential that it remained secret. Antoine knew that the doctor would never have imparted the information, because he too was handsomely rewarded, so the only other person that could have spilt the beans was Angelique's doctor friend Melany. She was on duty the day he went in for the transplant, and he hadn't recognised her at the time. Some time later, he remembered that she belonged to the ladies' club at the castle, and she was Angelique's best friend. Unfortunately he needed to get her off the map, but apparently he had waited too long. He realised that the damage was already done, and it was too late. He should have wiped her out immediately, and no one would have ever found out. Only this time Angelique reacted hastily, with so much anger, that she denied him of the most valuable pride. If she had done something less aggressive, he would have understood that she hated him after what he'd done to her daughter, but she had gone much too far, so all the love he had for Angelique had turned into hate. That is when he set out to destroy everything she loved; he was totally obsessed with destroying her.

Indra found out about all the things that Antoine had done secretly, by getting to know all the people he used to do the jobs. Indra was horrified after she had found out about the gruesome things he did and got away with. He made other people pay for his crimes, so she decided to give him a taste of his own medicine. Indra intended to take revenge, and she had the right cards to play with, and Antoine wouldn't even know that she was behind it. She worked closely with him, and ensured that she was in on anything he was planning. For every price he paid, she was prepared to double the amount for the crime to be reversed. For example, he had paid some people to bomb the winery, and Indra had informed Angelique, so she allowed them to plant the dummy bomb and make an artificial fire, for proof that they had done their jobs, and she instructed them to bomb his house instead, with all its contents he cherished.

On another occasion he hired Jack to pour caustic soda over Angelique's face and disfigure her, but Indra knew about the scheme and made sure that she was with her that day, and Jack was about to do so when he recognised Indra. Jack pulled back, and she asked him to protect Angelique instead of harming her.

When Antoine was locked up in the cave, it was Indra who left him there, while he wore only a skimpy short-sleeved T-shirt and shorts. She made sure that he had nothing to eat or drink and it was freezing cold in there. He would never have known that she had anything to do with it because she pretended not to know what the cave looked like. She had done this to make him feel what Leonardo could have gone through if he wasn't as intelligent as he was. Antoine was so obsessed with ruining Eric, that he framed his own accidents: with the electrical appliances, and the brake failure, the bad notes and the graffiti on his walls.

Indra explained that she let all the people he used blackmail him and get him to pay considerable amounts of money. She used his own money to buy back the company for her father to run, while she wanted to make him suffer for the things he'd done to everyone around him. She staged everything from the first crime he committed, and she got him to feel what it was like being raped, by six strong homosexuals, and then she set him up to feel what it was like to gulp dirty river water when someone tried to drown you, to be locked up in a cave and have no food or water in winter. She had known all along what his intentions were, so she got them to blow his own home instead of that of his brother. She had brought in all the ex-convicts he used to pull off the jobs to retaliate and blackmail him, until he had no more money to fend for himself.

She had taken his money and paid a better sum to reverse his crimes, when she came across his notes in the blue room, apparently the same notes Mrs Lemoin found which he had hidden in Calicorne, with all the pictures of Angelique and Anemone. He was so obsessed with his love for Angelique that he did not realise when things were getting out of hand. Indra knew that she had to stop somewhere along the line, and she decided that she wanted to draw the line when she had done all she thought possible, knowing that all would come out, because she no longer wanted the blood to continue, because he had got very close to killing Angelique and Eric, and she didn't want that on her conscience. She left him, knowing that this was the last straw. She punished him by taking Antonio, and used him as a weapon, and she played dirty tricks on him, ticking off things that he had done in the past, killing people, and he just went insane.

After Indra had concluded the account, she apologised that things had to get as far as it did, but she needed to put an end to all the pain, for everyone, and for Murielle, who had paid very dearly, with years of imprisonment. She added that she didn't order his death at anytime. She could have done it, but he was already doomed. After everyone had heard, it was very hard to believe what Indra had said, and everyone was surprised. Naturally, no one would have guessed that he could have actually got away with everything he had done, but they soon realised that Indra had spoken the truth, as Antoine just sat there and didn't defend himself.

Eric was completely dumbstruck, and he thought that there must have been an explanation for all the accusations Indra had directed at his brother; there was no way that his brother was capable of doing such things. Over the years

Antoine had always been present, he helped them out in many ways. Eric refused to believe it, and asked Antoine to defend himself and tell them that they were mistaken, but Antoine simply stared at him and shook his head. Then Eric realised that it was true. Eric was hysterical, and they had to keep him away from Antoine or he would have shot him right there, so he turned to Angelique, and enquired why she hadn't told him about it, and why she had suffered in silence, and never let him know what was happening. Why didn't anyone tell him what Antoine had done to Anemone?

Angelique explained that she had already taken the law into her own hands by taking away his pride and managing to keep him away from the castle, but she couldn't tell him about it. She knew that he would have reacted hastily, and his mother had been suffering from a heart ailment, and it would have upset her to the extent that she would have had another heart attack that would have been fatal and she couldn't handle to have that on her conscience. She told him that she knew how much he cared for Antoine although she didn't give a hoot. It was only because his mum would have found out, had he known, so she kept it to herself. Angelique told him that she had sometimes thought of ways to get him out of the way, but she couldn't think of something good enough. The rape story kept him away for quite a while. She said that every time he came close to her she freaked, and it occurred to her that when she was younger he had tried to take advantage of her several times. Then she remembered that Indra had told her to talk about all the bad things that had happened in her life, and that it was better to get things off her chest. She opened up to Indra, not knowing that she was dealing with Miss Sherlock Holmes. She said that she would never have thought Antoine capable of doing something as crazy as to rape his own niece, but when she realised that he did she snapped, and only thought of one way justice could be done, and she did it without regret.

Eric was silent when he walked over to his brother. Everyone looked on when he said, after slapping his brother in the face, 'This is for the day you beat me up to a pulp at the Fourbourg wedding.' Eric slapped him about seven times while saying, 'Take this you bastard. I'm going to kill you, for murdering my son in his own home, for raping my little girl and my wife, for killing the Polish lady and the young man in the gym, for killing Dad and selling his company to the enemy to save your ass, for killing Melany, Mr and Mrs du Preez and their son, Marc, and his best friend, Xavier. What about the man in the cubicle, and the two kids blown apart in Marc's car? And for the sadistic manner you killed the animals, and lastly for killing Mum; you caused her so much grieve that she clung on to dear life to try and save your butt, and you managed to kill her anyway.'

Giovanni pulled him away from Antoine, before he caused too much damage to Antoine's face. He spat at Antoine and told him that he was lucky that his mum wanted him to be present when they put on the video that she had made. They started the video. Edwina, looked very sad. Under normal circumstances she would have been telling them not to cry, but she seemed to know that they weren't only mourning her death, but Antoine's life.

She started by saying, 'I know what you all must be going through at this moment, and I am certainly only a small part of your grievances. I'm going to be brief, there is no point in rubbing salt in the wound, so I'll get right down to it. It would be less painful if you had all discovered it by yourselves, but I still have a duty to fulfil towards my family, so I asked Antoine to come forward and admit to all the bad things he had done in the past, because he stands guilty before you all.

'Angelique and Eric have been very strong to have come through the traumatic circumstances, and still stand firm. I'm not making excuses for Antoine, but his crimes started out as passionate, and just got out of hand. Antoine had never had the least love in his heart for Eric, and by God I sure tried to make him accept things, and just when I thought that he did, I realised that I had made the biggest mistake of my life by trusting him. I know and I've always known that Antoine was out to destroy you. He never liked you, but I prayed that things would change. I knew from the day that you fell in love with Angelique that Antoine would hate you all the more. I wouldn't like to go into detail if you are aware; if not, you've got to listen carefully.

'This message is for you, Antoine, from your mum who loves you. We've always loved you, both your father and I. I forgive you for what you've done. I've been aware of your ungodly acts, and now, my son, I want you to tell everyone about all the awful things you have done. Obviously, not everyone has it in their hearts to forgive, let alone to forget. You've made innocent people suffer and die, but I wouldn't like you to rot in jail. I would like you to know that I've found all your black diaries, and read them in detail. I could not believe that I brought a monster into the world. It is clear for all to see that there is no end to the pain you endure. You know that you'll be going to jail for your acts, but there is no way that you can stop yourself from harming the people who once loved you. I've thought about what would be good for you, son, so I wrote a personal letter addressed to you only. You can excuse yourself from the company and read it, and then join the others. What I suggest is an act of love for you and all concerned.

'I've forgiven you, because you're my son and I brought you up. I'll always love you, no matter what you've done in the past, and remember that everybody loved you, but there is no longer a place for you with the people you're gathered with today.

'Now that you all know, I rest my soul in peace, and thank God that freedom has finally struck my family. God bless you Angelique and Eric. Indra and your children, may God bless you too. Was it worthwhile? Love has no value when it isn't returned and you cannot put a price tag to it. These are the things that happen when love turns to hate.'

Antoine opened the letter and read the contents; then he removed something from the envelope. When he got back he was in tears. He knew that it was all over for him. He clutched the letter in the palm of his hand and came back in while everyone was chatting. The police had come on the scene to take him away, but before they could do so he asked them to give him some time with Romeo. He removed his ring from his finger and gave it to him. He later called Antonio, and told him that he loved him, and that he never wanted to harm him.

Antoine insisted that he wanted them to know why he did what he did. He loved Angelique, and she chose his brother above him. She gave Eric a son, knowing that he desired to have one of his own with her, because she was his life. He hated Eric for getting everything his heart desired, even the castle. As a little boy he already dreamed of the fairy-tale life he was going to have with Angelique and their children, but Eric always spoiled everything, and he had so much pleasure out of seeing Eric down in the dumps. He never intended to hurt Anemone, but when he saw that there was no way he could get close to Angelique, he snapped and took it out on Anemone. He asked Indra to forgive him, but he just used her to satisfy his sexual desires, though it did change when she got pregnant. When he found out it was a girl she was carrying, it had no significance whatsoever, but everything changed when

Antonio was born, but it was a little too late because he already had Romeo.

All of a sudden, Antoine was having difficulty breathing, and Indra got him a glass of water, but he started getting pale, and uttered some words while he was choking.

He looked at Angelique, and managed to say, 'Angel, please forgive me, I love you, I've done everything because I loved you and I knew that you loved my brother, and for that I hated him. Please, you've got to tell me that you forgive me.'

Angelique, seeing that he was a dying man, immediately promised that she'd forgiven him and then he died. Everyone was amazed; they tried to understand what could have been written in the letter, and that was surely what made him commit suicide. Eric read the letter, and tears streamed down his face.

Yes, Antoine, you've guessed correctly. You cannot go through life regretting all the bad things you've done. You've made everyone suffer, including yourself, for the sake of the love of someone who already belonged to someone else. Angelique suffered along with your brother, while you were destroying their lives. You say that you love Angelique, but she had to pay the price when you took advantage of her children. How could you have done something so cruel? You hated your brother; no one could have forced you to love him. By God I've tried to make you change. You're going to have to take a decision right now, whether you want to continue making Angelique's life a misery. She has paid very dearly. There is only one other alternative: take your life and ask God to forgive you, my son, because if you don't someone else will. Do this for the one you love, my son.

If you go to jail, you'll be tortured, and God alone knows what will happen to you next. Remember, only because I love you I want to save you from the dark world out there. I hope that you will find peace with yourself, and may God forgive you for what you've done. We've all sinned, but God always forgives, so pray to God and may your soul rest in peace.

Mummy and Daddy

Eric wept. He had never realised that Antoine loved Angelique the way he did. He didn't even know that Antoine hated him and regarded him as a rival instead of a brother. He was so sad because he couldn't even accommodate one little wish that Antoine was after, and now it was too late, he had taken his own life. What was even more sad was that just before he died he wanted to get his rifle and pull the trigger on his brother who had killed his son, the brother he would never have thought capable of such a thing. His mother was right: if Antoine had to go to jail, he would have ordered Eric's death; it was clear that he wasn't going to give up. There were some people out there who would have killed him anyway, even Eric would have pulled the trigger, but his mother saved him from committing an act he might have regretted.

Three days later Antoine was buried at the castle, and so were the bad memories. There was no more living in fear. They were going to make up for lost time and live the way they always dreamed of. Eric and Angelique went on a second honeymoon to the Comoros for eight long weeks, and visited the mountains that had taken her parents' lives.

Anemone minded Leonardo, Leandra and Angelo, who was doing a swell thing with Enrique and Romeo, who always looked upon himself as the chief. He had somehow taken Antoine's place; they were alike in many ways, and he would always trigger off a remembrance of his father he knew nothing about, but some things were better left unsaid, and he was completely ignorant in this regard.

When they buried Antoine, they buried his secrets and the bad things along with him; they held on only to the good.

Pedro had grown up and matured in the meantime. He realised how much he had hurt Indra in the past and knew that he actually loved her. He made up for all the lost time, and they had a baby boy straightaway. He learnt how to love children and he made a great job of it. He treated her like a queen. Pedro had become great friends with his brother-in-law Paolo, so they often got together and things were working out just great. Indra had inherited Mountain's Peak, the only thing that Antoine had left. They planned to take a vacation at Mountains Peak and invited Murielle along with their two little daughters they had adopted in Brazil. Mr and Mrs Fourbourg came along too and everyone was glad the nightmare was finally over and done with.

As for Mr Fourbourg, business was booming to the extent that he could do with a break. He got his sons-in-law to run his business while he travelled with his wife, exactly the same as Eric had done. Giovanni kept an eye on the business while his father-in-law went and saw all the islands they could possibly dream of, in the company of their friends, Mr and Mrs Mancheta.

Melany's husband remained good friends with Eric, and often played golf with him. For many months he mourned his wife's tragic death, but he later met Norma, and became very friendly towards the aerobics instructor at the castle club. He joined the club that had since become a unisex club, and they arranged tours to other countries. He fell in love with Norma, who got pregnant, and he planned to marry her as soon as possible and was happy to have his first son too. He never had any children with Melany.

Mrs Mancheta and her husband, Franco, lived in the same home in Calicorne, where the doctor opened up his own private practice, while her two boys, Jason and Keanan were happily married. Then they died tragically in a car accident, after they tried to renew their love of drugs for fun. Jason was driving when he hit an oncoming carrier, killing the six of them instantly – they had their little ones along with them on this fatal trip. Mrs Mancheta was completely heartbroken for her sons, but there was nothing she could do to bring them back. She just thanked the Lord that her son, Giovanni, had turned out to be a great kid. She was proud of him, and she had Enrique and Romeo. Anemone had a little girl on the way, and they couldn't have asked for anything more out of life.

Recently André had brought his son to see Angelique. When he introduced his wife to her she thought that she was dreaming: the woman was identical to Deline, and they had two children of their own. She later found out that Daphné was Deline's identical twin, and she was sure that Deline would have blessed this marriage and was looking over them.

Romeo turned out to be a great kid, and the truth about his identity was kept in the strictest confidence, although somehow, he resembled his father, and filled his place at the castle. He seemed very interested in the fine arts of the castle, and he was the one who explored all the time, until one day he came across some boxes covered in spider webs, and, as he was a inquisitive boy, he carried on and with the help of his Uncle Leonardo and Uncle Angelo, he opened up about six boxes that contained a treasure so rare that they were going to make a fortune. They were very excited and called their parents. It turned out to be a treasure that dated from the sixteenth century and was very valuable. They had lost a lot of their family but they recovered the lost family jewels, and everything else that went along with them – happiness.

Indra wrote a book about her life and that of the Lemoin family, and had it published, even though the Lemoin family had asked her not to. They felt that they'd endured enough and suffered even to think of the hurt it would cause Romeo and everyone else. It was a passionate crime that turned from love to hate and left Antoine Lemoin obsessively destructive. The book turned out to be a bestseller.